HOW TO BE A FRENCH GIRL

How to be a French Girl

ROSE CLEARY

WEATHERGLASS BOOKS

For my dad,
who saved us both the
inevitable mutual embarrassment by
passing away before this was published.

LONDON

Southend Central station. Toes to the yellow line. Staring at the tracks below. More commuters, more bodies, gathering. A train arrives. It feels serendipitous when the train doors slide open directly before her, as though she has not deliberately chosen the same spot as yesterday, the day before, the day before, the day before, or the day before.

She sits in a window seat, facing against the direction of travel. The past disappears before her. In around fifty-seven minutes she will step off the train into London. After seven months of this routine, twice a day, five days a week, she has stopped believing the train is going anywhere. The view from the window is instead a simulation, and she never escapes the city where she works nor the city where she lives. The train is a shuttle of false time.

Her body settles, flesh adjusting. Commuters pack in. Outside the window she spots wildlife. Picking out pheasants' round browns. Briefly catching rabbits motionless in straw.

Messages on her phone from unsaved numbers.

Hellooo the hotel is booked, 250 for our special night devil emoji *could you send me half the money asap xx*

She blocks the number.

Okay I am going to be really honest with you even though you don't deserve it. But you seem to be ignoring all my messages so please allow me this for at least a sense of closure. I thought we had something. If I knew you were gonna ghost me then I wouldn't have slept with you. Wish you had been honest about your intentions. And yes, I have given much thought that your radio silence might be, just might be, that you are afraid of your feelings—

She blocks the number.

yo wyd

Blocks the number. Thumb hovering, she opens Bumble.

Lorenzo, 42

Daniel, 20

Paul, 24

Jez, 43

Matthew, 36

Javier, 25

Javier. She presses his face with her thumb. Two years younger than her. Dark hair. White teeth. Spanish or southern European. His photos suggest an *outgoing personality type*. Standing on a mountain, arms raised. Wearing a white T-shirt at a festival.

She sends him a message: *Hola Javier! Enjoying the sunshine?*

Immediately afterwards she closes the app and slips her phone back into her bag.

She looks out of the window. From behind tall greenery the sun emerges, beaming directly into her eyes.

An artificial plant gives the illusion of oxygen. The front of the building is glass. She sits behind the reception desk, staring at the buildings across the street, which are also made of glass. The buildings reflect each other and everything between them. Her email inbox contains forty-five emails in total, all read.

People arrive through the glass wall in *office wear*. They walk past the artificial plant, past the reception desk, past her – the receptionist – and step heavily up a flight of black metal stairs which wind above her head, to where their desks await them on the first floor. Their phone calls and banter drop down through the air.

I know you were an art student and you've got an interest in the creative field, the recruitment consultant had said, but I think you'll really like this place. It's B2B, do you know what that is? As you can imagine, it's quite high-end. But these guys have a really cool and laid-back ethos and an open-plan office and it's temp-to-perm for the right person.

In the office kitchen she stands with her back against the wall and eats four custard creams, one by one: pulling the top layer off, then scraping the cream centre with her front teeth before eating the bottom layer. Repeating this for all four biscuits systematically.

She takes a fifth biscuit to the reception desk, sits down, and puts it in her mouth whole. Wills the biscuit to break down in her saliva as she dissociates in front of her computer monitor.

The reception phone rings.

She begins chewing, mouth moving quickly. Pushing what remains of the biscuit into her left cheek, she picks up the phone and says, with a near-motionless face, Good afternoon, Datata.

She is two minutes away from the bar where she arranged to meet Javier at 19:00. She stands and flicks between social media apps until 19:05, then puts her phone back into her bag, straightens her shoulders and walks into the bar. The interior is exposed brick and metal stools. Cutlery in buckets. The staff are bored and young. A tweet she saw at some point crosses her mind: *there's a fine line between chic and shit*. One thousand, seven hundred likes, four hundred and sixty-two retweets.

Someone who looks like Javier is hunched over a phone at a table. Spotting her, he stands and air-kisses her on both cheeks, stubble grazing her skin. He is shorter than he appeared in his photos and has a nose piercing. He gestures for her to sit opposite. The stool is high up and awkward to climb onto.

She asks what he is drinking, not in order to buy him another but to stop him staring at her.

He looks down at his drink as though he had forgotten it was there. Oh. I think you are going to laugh at me because it is a female drink, he says. He has a Spanish accent.

She asks what a *female drink* is.

You promise not to laugh at me?

She raises an eyebrow and thinks about how easy it is to create sexual tension with a stranger.

Javier waits a few more seconds before saying, Malibu and Coke. Then he sits back heavily as though this was a monumental admission, smile flashing. He talks about how he gets bored of drinking beer and that he had a conversation with his friend about it as he did not know what to drink when he met her tonight, so...

She stops listening. Javier's casting of any drink as a female drink, and his apparent embarrassment and his excuse, has annoyed her. She orders a large red wine. Javier tries to maintain a high level of energy and dominates the conversation. Head on hand, widening her eyes and laughing at the right moments, she lets it roll over her.

Another bar. They sit outside. She lights a cigarette and it becomes a prop in her hand, a gesticular aid. She starts talking more. Their voices get louder. People turn to look at them – *this cool and interesting couple, smoking cigarettes and talking fervently*, she hopes, although she also hopes that they agree *she is cooler and more interesting than him*. On her fifth glass of wine and his third vodka and orange, him having changed drinks somewhere, she brings up Catalonian independence. He tips up his glass to drain it completely, eyes heavier than before.

So you don't live in London? he asks.

She comes to consciousness from beneath a layer of nausea. The sensation of a warm body beside her, the back of a neck with sparse black down. She sits up, locates yesterday's clothes from around the room, turns her underwear inside out. Finds the bathroom. Locks the door. She stares at herself in the mirror. Thin film of grease. Acne scars irritated from alcohol and cigarettes. Sore eyes boring into sore eyes. Red lines from rough bedding mark her chest like welts from a whip. The sink is cold against her stomach. She uses her weight against it to push the rounded flesh back.

She turns on the tap and splashes her face with cold water. It spills on the floor. She squeezes toothpaste onto an index finger and rubs it over her teeth, reaching a small hole which has appeared in a distant back tooth. She takes out her finger and wedges the tip of her tongue into the tooth, feeling its decay. She opens her mouth, wet and foamy jaw wide, angling to see the cavity. It is too far back. She fills her mouth directly from the cold water tap and spits it out, rubbing her face and mouth dry on a hand towel which is already damp. She decides to ignore her reflection for the rest of the day.

Holding her phone before her, neck bent, she follows Google Maps to the Underground station and increases the radius on Tinder.

Russell, 37

A mountain in the background. Brown curly hair on a balding scalp. Black sunglasses.

Kwaku, 44

Photo taken from a low angle. Poor-quality image, pixelated.

D-Zed, 23

What a name. Sports vest. Long chin.

Jeremy, 26

Pink shirt. Sitting beside a girl, sharing a sideways look. She wonders why he included this photo.

Jeremy, again, this time *39.*

Standing so far in the distance that his face is blurred. Lycra cycling shorts.

Tomasz, 45

Winston, 19

Jonathan, 32

Hugo, 25

Andrew, 43

After a while she no longer registers the distinguishing details between profiles.

She sits behind the reception desk with a headache. Someone arrives for a lunch meeting with Oscar, whose email signature says he is Sales Director. His visitor stands and looks awkward while she picks up the phone and dials Oscar's extension. After around twenty seconds, Oscar walks down the stairs, shakes the person's hand and slaps them on the back.

Catering all set up? he says to her on his way to the boardroom.

She nods once. Double-clicks something. Pretends to be busy.

The meeting room walls are entirely glass, frosted down to the middle, leaving the bottom half visible. People inside become all legs.

Twelve minutes later, Jerry, the Managing Director, walks down the stairs and into an empty meeting room. He turns and asks without looking at her, Where are the guys?, but does not stop walking and enters the boardroom before she can answer. Before the door closes, she hears him say, Gentlemen, good afternoon.

The reception phone rings. It is Oscar, calling her from the boardroom, asking her to bring coffees. One white with sugar, one white without sugar, one black with sugar. The deep notes of his voice come through the glass wall.

A machine makes the coffee. She bites a thumbnail then places all the coffees on a tray and carries it to the boardroom, pushing the door open with her back. The sandwiches she set up earlier – an *artisan sandwich platter*: half meat, half vegetarian, half prosciutto, half chickpea, ordered from a new caterer in Borough Market and which she had spent three minutes positioning on the table as symmetrically as possible – are untouched.

An hour later the boardroom door opens and Jerry walks out alongside the client, hands in his pockets. Unvaried, she hears him say. The catering had been a little *unvaried*.

She waits for them to leave the office before standing and going into the boardroom to tidy it. The artisan sandwich platter remains untouched. Oscar is still sitting there, a menthol-scented vape crackling in his mouth. As she begins to collect half-empty coffee cups, she catches it, there: the telltale mark of one sandwich thumbed, moist triangle sides parted, contents exposed and inspected before being abandoned.

Just a little bit of advice, Oscar is saying. When you've got clients waiting in reception, try talking to them. Make conversation. Ask them how their day is going. Yeah?

In her kitchen in Southend which is not a kitchen but a domain eked out by the placement of furniture to give the illusion that it is separate from her bedroom, two large saucepans rumble with heat on the stove. Pasta and a tomato sauce, the cheapest and easiest meal she can prepare in bulk. A flash of childhood memory: having a bath filled with water boiled from the kettle for an unknown reason, something like the central heating being cut off. Too poor. The space behind that memory is empty, in its place something emerging that she read on the internet a few months ago: *Real Italians always add a pinch of sugar to their tomato dish.* She finds a crumpled bag of caster sugar and sprinkles it into the tomato sauce. The fact that she is not Italian is irrelevant.

Her phone sounds a notification. A message pops up.

Alexis.

so you're not going to entertain me…

She ignores it. Scrolls more profiles.

Harry, 32.

Dirty blonde hair, open shirt. Surferesque in a way which seems decades old.

She writes a message: *Good evening ;) is that a beer in your hand or are you just pleased to see me…?*

She reads it back to herself, judging whether her use of a well-known phrase works on a semantic level. She sends it before scrolling through her unread messages.

You matched with Freddie!

You matched with Lee-Sam! She opens the profile of Lee-Sam. Glasses. On his profile he has self-described himself as a music producer.

She writes him a message: *Hey… want to talk dirty?*

He replies six minutes later: *Not that kind of guy…*

She closes the message, opening the profile of Freddie. Shaved head.

Hey… want to talk dirty?

He replies in two minutes: *Hello gorgeous… never say no is my Motto xx What You wearing*

She looks down, considering her damp coat. Wet Primark flats. Black tights.

Well at the moment I'm wearing my secretary gear… I'm all wet so I have to take it all off… want to help me?

This exchange goes back and forth for five minutes, developing into more graphic language, each describing the various positions they could have sex in, what furniture they could do it against. He sends her a photo of his penis.

So hard for You right now…

She doesn't doubt that this picture has likely been taken at some point in the past and is now his go-to erection photo. His upper thighs are coated with wiry blonde hair.

what Would you like me to Do with This gorgeous??

She closes the photo. The thought of his leg hair is for some reason more powerful than the main subject of the picture. More messages come before she can respond.

Show me your Pussy then

Another one.

Send me a Photo

She considers what the benefits of doing this would be for her. The conversation is growing boring. They have discussed doggy style, deep throating and so on. He sends another message. It is a video of him masturbating. She turns her phone volume down to mute, watching the video politely until he ejaculates.

He sends another message: *Your Turn now.*

Her mouth tastes dense and metallic. The messages keep coming.

come on i Want to see you Pleasure yourself

Or do u want me To come over there and Fuck you right now

you in southend yeah? Whereabouts

let me come over there

so ready to ruin u

She goes to Freddie's profile and selects *Block this user.*
Are you sure you want to block this user?
Yes.

You have a new match! The new match is *Silas, 35.* Varying degrees of beard in each photo.

... and that's me, Silas finishes, grinning nervously.

She nods once, feeling her eyelids drooping. Right, right, she murmurs, bringing her wine glass to her lips.

In a crevice between buildings two hours and three minutes later, she shoves her hands into his trousers, wanking him rapidly. His knees buckle. He clenches his fists, repeatedly looking to the street.

She hisses in his ear, Stop fucking looking. No one gives a shit.

Her phone alarm goes off at 06:00 and she wakes immediately. It feels as though all her muscles have been pulled. Pushing herself into a sitting position, she opens her phone. A message appears at the top of the screen – Javier.

I feel terrible for not being awake when you left. So, i'm sorry. Can i make it up to you? Are you free this week? x

She rereads it three times, squidging her tongue into the cavity at the back of her mouth. A sudden and new sensitivity makes her withdraw. She remembers that after work she has arranged to meet Jenny, a friend from college who remained in Southend and did not go to art school like she did. Jenny, who took an essentially militant stand against the *institutionalizing and exploitation of young artists*, a stand which has remained an undercurrent in their relationship.

For no particular reason, she sends Jenny a vague and non-committal message about not being available. Jenny responds immediately, offering to reschedule to Saturday. She closes the conversation and puts her phone face down. Bites a fingernail. Picks up her phone again and opens YouTube. In the thumb-nail list of suggested videos there is one entitled *The Girl with Half a Face*. She selects it. A documentary about a woman with half of her face gone, as though dissolved beneath the skin, half-resembling a skull, one mascaraed eye hanging heavily. There are comparative shots between her school graduation photo and her current appearance. The dull hum of a nasal voice-over threads the images together: the woman lies on a hospital bed, her graduation photo, looming slowly, growing larger on the screen; the woman is in a hospital bed again, being fed through a tube; present day, the woman sitting on her front porch, terrible rictus grin.

The brown water of the estuary slips past. She catches the tail of some small creature as it hides itself beneath shrubbery. The train window begins to fill with grey, yellow, green, blue, grey, grey, more grey. Then Fenchurch Street station.

From behind the reception desk she sees movement outside the office window. Three men. The one wearing a grey suit she recognizes as someone she has taken a dislike to, but she cannot remember why.

The men enter the office and approach the reception desk.

Grey Suit says, I'm here with the guys from Op-Us. We have a meeting with Jerry.

She gestures towards the boardroom and Grey Suit says loudly, Great.

The three men walk towards the room. One turns and says thank you over his shoulder.

His indeterminate accent intrigues her. She stares at the back of his head and feels the urge to speak.

Do you. Do you need coffee?

Grey Suit holds a takeaway coffee cup aloft. We're great, he calls back.

The three men enter the boardroom and close the door.

She picks up the phone and dials Jerry's extension. It rings for one minute. Jerry appears at the top of the stairs and begins clattering down towards her. She puts down the phone and says, They're in—

Appearing not to hear her, Jerry walks straight into the meeting room opposite the stairs. He sees that the room is empty and turns on his heel.

They're in the boardroom, she says.

Jerry strides into the boardroom, finding the men inside and saying, Gentlemen, good morning. She watches as Jerry's short legs do a circuit around the table, greeting the occupants in turn before marching back to the door, which opens. His face appears and he looks at her for the first time that morning. Could you get these guys a coffee?

Don't worry about it, Grey Suit shouts from inside the room. We're great.

She sits and stares for two minutes. Eventually she decides to water the artificial plant by the reception desk, hoping that someone will see her doing this and talk to her about it. About how *quirky* and *interesting* she is. The water rises above the fake pebble bed, then overflows.

Sitting on a stone bench in a park square, she opens a Tupperware filled with cold pasta, forking it into her mouth with one hand, phone held in the other. No messages.

As she walks back down the road to the office, she sees the two men from Op-Us standing outside, facing in her direction. The two men mirror each other: side by side, smoking cigarettes. One of them is tall, with narrow shoulders, reddish *flyaway* hair, shuffling and talking distractedly to the other one. The other one is looking at her. She estimates he is five foot nine. Feet planted apart, he is facing her with his whole body. His biceps are visible under a white shirt tightly tucked into his jeans. Wide nose. Big eyes. Dark pupils. Strong brow line. There is something about his face, as though he is about to smile or speak. But instead he brings his cigarette to his mouth. Clips it deftly between his lips. The smoke leaves his nostrils in two steady streams. His eyes still do not leave her. Something about his gaze does not produce in her the usual twist of irritation, the irk. His stare is a fact. When she realizes the man with red hair is also staring at her, the familiar irk of being ogled by strange men returns. She looks away and walks into the office, pretending not to have seen either of them.

She lies in bed for twelve minutes before her phone alarm goes off at 06:00. It begins raining as soon as she leaves her flat. Without stopping, she feels inside her bag for an umbrella. It is not there. She folds her arms, bows her head and walks faster.

At 07:27 the train arrives and she takes her usual window seat. There is an advert on the wall at the end of the carriage. She reads the slogan once, then again, and again and again. TIME'S UP! For _Hay Fever_. TIME'S UP! For _Hay Fever_. TIME'S UP! For _Hay Fever_. TIME'S UP! For _Hay Fever_. TIME'S UP! For _Hay Fever_. TIME'S UP! For _Hay Fever_. TIME'S UP! For _Hay Fever_. TIME'S UP! For _Hay Fever_. TIME'S UP! For _Hay Fever_. TIME'S UP! For _Hay Fever_. TIME'S UP! For _Hay Fever_. TIME'S UP! For _Hay Fever_. TIME'S UP! For _Hay Fever_. TIME'S UP! For _Hay Fever_. TIME'S UP! For _Hay Fever_.

She opens Javier's profile, sliding between his photos. White T-shirt. Sitting on the shoulders of another man, at a gig, both sweating. Riding a donkey.

The train stops at the next station and another commuter sits beside her. This is unnecessary because there are other seats available. She can hear him breathing. Hrrffffffff hhhhh-hhhh. She turns to the window. The odour of trousers worn three days in a row. She closes her eyes. Hrrffffffff hhhhhhhhh. Hrrffffffff hhhhhhhhh. The speed of the train is too hollow a sound to drown it out. Hrrffffffff hhhhhhhhh.

Could you sit somewhere else.

Her voice cracks through the hush of the carriage.

The man's face looks soft. Caught out.

You're breathing too loudly, she says.

He blinks at her. Mouth opening. Saying uuuuuhhhhhhhhh.

Sit anywhere else. An indicative gesture with her head and neck. There's loads of room.

Sorry, he mumbles.

Once he moves, she writes a message to Javier.

Jerry sends an email to everyone in the office. It's marked *High Importance* and says that Data have signed Op-Us as their new European partner. Something something about being market leaders in France and Germany, and Data would be their first UK distributors. Exciting times, etc.

Hadrien and Gus will be here over the next week or so to get familiar with our fantastic operation. Please make them feel welcome.

She googles *hadrien op-us*. A LinkedIn profile is among the search results. Hadrien Auger, Regional Sales Manager. The one with red hair and slight shoulders.

She types: *gus op-us*. Gustave Caron, European Sales Director. No photo. Previous employment: Finitarium, Activari. Education: a school name in French. Paris. Graduated:1999.

Someone from Marketing descends the stairs behind her and comes around to the reception desk. Purple hair styled into *loose waves*. Could you post these for me, please? Sorry, I know it's raining. Marketing births several parcels from her arms onto the reception desk. Thanks, she says. Also, could you book the boardroom for the whole of Monday? It's for Op-Us. Could you arrange some catering as well?

She glances at Marketing briefly and notices her *winged eye-liner*.

Sorry, I know it's like, literally Thursday, but we only just got the confirmation.

It's fine, she says.

Great, so there'll be Oscar's team, so that's four. And then Op-Us, and then Roman, so. Seven people. Just, like, a normal breakfast spread. And then for lunch—

Sandwiches.

Perfect, yes. And then also could you—

Set up the tea and coffee.

You know all this by heart now! Thanks so much.

She sighs too loudly. Marketing doesn't appear to have heard and walks away back up the stairs.

To decompress from this exchange, she stares at her computer monitor for twelve minutes before standing to gather the packages. The reception phone rings. Jerry's name appears. Arms full, she picks up the handset and balances it on her shoulder.

Is the boardroom free on Monday?

It's booked for Op-Us.

Could you organize catering?

Yeah, I—

Probably best to order enough for six or seven people, Jerry says. Maybe just some pastries, fruit and yoghurt for breakfast. We would like lunch as well. Could you get sandwiches?

She blinks.

Are you writing this down?

Yep, she responds.

Then also if you could be there to do coffee.

Okay.

Fabulous.

She hangs up and takes packages to the post office and stares at another girl in the queue, possibly her age, and decides that they're wearing too much make-up.

—

At Pret a Manger her debit card is declined. This has happened before. The person behind the counter communicates this soft-ly-softly, as though it is anyone's fault but her own. This annoys her. She tries again, this time pressing the card into the slot of the contactless pad, sure she has not yet reached her overdraft limit. The payment is accepted. She feels her face burning as she marches out onto the street. A film of rain on the ground reflects the buildings and the sky.

Locking herself in the office toilet, she holds her shoes under the hand dryer.

When she comes back to reception, the desk phone displays two missed calls. Each call is from Oscar's extension. As she goes to dial his number back, he rings again.

You sound cheerful as always, he says. Oscar's desk is located close to the top of the stairs, so close that she can hear his voice echo above her from his desk. It even precedes its own arrival via phone. Have any catering arrangements have been made for—

Yes, she responds.

He asks if these have been made for breakfast and lunch, to which she says yes again.

In that case could you book us a table for seven o'clock at the Riverside?

He hangs up before she can.

She glances at her reflection in the glass wall. It feels like she is looking into an oversized fish tank display, with a miserable receptionist inside.

Outside a wine bar filled with people in suits, she pretends to read a *Guardian* article on her phone. The music from the bar can be heard outside.

Javier approaches wearing a military jacket. He presses his lips to her cheek. He is late.

Inside, the bar is busy. They stand beside each other without talking. A gap at the bar opens up and Javier pushes himself into it. She waits with folded arms, watching Javier's profile, wondering what the woman working behind the bar thinks of him. A man jostles her, treading on her toes. She pretends it is not happening. After seven minutes Javier appears with a glass of red wine and an exaggeratedly tall pint glass.

I got you your favourite, he says. Tips the wine glass towards her.

Javier must think her favourite wine is *red*. On Instagram, a sommelier turned influencer said that their favourite type of red wine was *that which tasted as though it had been mixed in an ashtray, coating the tongue like tar*. She found herself agreeing, although it was difficult to remember what her taste in red wine had been before.

She asks if they can sit outside.

Javier tilts his head to hear better. What? They are both shouting over the music.

Outside.

The garden is a terraced patio lit with fairy lights. There is loud chattering and obnoxious laughter. They move wordlessly towards an empty table covered in half-finished drinks. Javier moves each glass to the other end of the bench.

She sits and puts her bag on the bench beside her. Feels Javier's eyes on her.

You have such a big bag, he says. Are you always carrying everything with you?

She reaches for her glass, inhaling acidity, artificial cranberries. A bottle of this wine costs six pounds in her local supermarket. I don't carry *everything*, she says.

Having finished clearing the table, Javier sits and rests his head on his hand and asks how her day was.

Fine.

You were at work?

I work every day. Monday to Friday. Full-time.

Where do you work?

She frowns. I told you before.

He rubs his eyes. Right, right… I'm sorry. You did. I just forgot. But you are an artist as well?

I stopped being an artist when I left art school.

His white teeth flash. I remember now. You were a painter?

Sculptor. She folds her arms. Unfolds them again. But I can paint, she adds.

What about where you are from. It is far from here?

It's just a shithole, she says, shrugging. A shithole by the sea.

Why is that?

Nothing goes on there. And the sea water is brown.

Pulling out a packet of cigarettes, she holds it open to him. He shakes his head. She puts one in her mouth. Paws in her bag for a lighter. Javier is holding one towards her. She hesitates, then leans in. He lights it and says, Chivalry isn't dead, no?

She exhales quickly in order to respond. Chivalry is a traditional masculine concept which perpetuates outdated gender dynamics, she says.

Javier sits back. I can tell that you are an artist.

What does that mean?

I just know.

Artist is a broad term.

Okay, I'll tell you how I know. He flicks his eyes down the parts of her body that are visible from behind the table. You're wearing all black. And the way you have your hair… It's unusual.

I don't do it on purpose. It just goes like this.

Alright. I'm just saying that… When I first saw you, I thought there was something different about you. And when you said that you were an artist, it made sense.

How, though? Artists aren't, like, *special*.

Javier picks at something stuck to the tabletop. I disagree, he says. You know, at home I was always the weird one. I watched old-school American horror movies, that kind of thing.

That's not weird.

Maybe. Maybe. But I was the only person who was interested in these things. I was different to everyone else. But then when I came here to London, everyone was different. So, I don't know. Maybe I am ordinary. But you, you are not.

She flicks her cigarette in an ashtray in a way that reveals to him that she is annoyed.

It is hard to know what you're thinking, he says.

You've literally met me twice, Javier. How are you supposed to know.

He grins quickly. You want to know what my favourite English word is? Melancholy.

Smoke runs out of her nose in mirth. He ignores it.

And when I look at you, I see that in your eyes.

She stubs out her half-finished cigarette on the bench. Oh, great. So you think I'm, what? *Sad?*

What I mean is… it's something about—

What you're saying, Javier, is that you've fucked me once and now you have some idealized conception of who I am.

Well—

Just some projection of me as a quirky little artist. She waggles her fingers with the words, then downs the rest of her wine.

Javier's eyes go wide like a wary cat. I don't mean to upset you, he says.

Don't worry. Apparently I'm sad anyway.

His hand is on hers now. She pulls away, grabs her bag and stands up, hearing Javier call her name as she pushes against people, crossing the patio and back into the bar, through the crowd, to the exit. She barges too hard against a man in a suit, who spins round and calls out, Alright love?

Fuck you.

She boards the 20:37 train at Fenchurch Street. She passes other office workers, alternately subdued or drunk and talking loudly, or hurriedly eating Burger King. There are no seats alone. She sits next to a man who is already snoring. In the dark, the window offers little except for the glowing orbs of lamp posts as the train pulls away. Her reflection looms white.

She walks through her front door. Still in her coat, she takes out her phone and opens Badoo. She swipes right on someone. Swipes right on the next one. Right again. Right. Right right right right rightrightrightrightrightright.

A match.

The other profile sends her a message: *What you looking for on here?*

She scratches her leg absent-mindedly with one hand, typing *I'm open-minded* with the other.

Does that mean you don't know? Tongue-out emoji

The tongue-out emoji is sick-making.

She blocks him. Her eyes refocus on her bed, the crumpled duvet. She moves around it towards her cupboard, hand reaching for something: a square of chocolate, a bottle of wine.

In bed she googles *gustave caron* again. Aside from his LinkedIn profile, one of the results is a Facebook profile, the privacy set so that only one photo is viewable. The image shows three men, arms around one another. Some hand gestures and grins.

With her thumb and forefinger she enlarges it, picking out the familiar face. Here Gustave looks unremarkable, or at least not how she remembers him.

A Google Images search. Gustave's professional headshot appears, multiplied. Something about his smile – at ease and commercial at the same time – is odd. She can barely look at it. The pages are populated by the Op-Us logo, graphics, stock imagery. On page four there is a photo of people at a conference, a crowd of mostly men watching a woman speak at a podium. She spots him standing furthest away from the camera, dark hair, dark eyebrows and dark chin seemingly enhanced by the distance. White shirt and black suit.

Friday morning. The train is late. While waiting on the platform in her usual spot, a woman has pressed into the space beside her. She watches the woman's left foot as it creeps towards the yellow line, pretending not to be pushing in.

The train eventually pulls in and the doors open.

Excuse me, she says, not meaning to be polite. Bends her elbow and uses it to jab into the woman's side. She steps past her and onto the train to take her usual seat, staring out of the window, pretending not to notice the woman glaring at her.

When she arrives at the office, a figure is standing at the reception desk. Dark hair cropped. Suit jacket. Leather laptop bag on the floor by his feet. One arm bent before him, possibly checking a watch. The man turns. She stops. It is Gustave Caron.

Can I help you?

I was hoping you would have a room for me? To work in, I mean. I have a meeting around the corner in a few hours and nowhere to go until then.

That room there, she says, pointing directly to meeting room three.

He follows her pointed finger. That room?

She nods.

He picks up his laptop, says thank you, and walks towards the room.

She puts down her bag and pulls out her chair, preparing to sit, but finds herself following Gustave to the meeting room doorway and watching him unpack his laptop.

Coffee? Her voice comes out strange and shrill, not hers.

I will get it myself, he says without looking up.

She lingers in the doorway, wanting him to look at her again. His scent fills the room. Cigarettes and sharp pine in blue. She realizes she is staring when he stops unpacking and looks up at her with an expression of polite expectancy. She blinks rapidly. I'll let Jerry know you're here?

He appears to consider this. It would be rude not to, he says with a slight smile. It feels conspiratorial. This makes her smile back. Then he busies himself again and it dawns on her that this is the end of the interaction and to press further would be to bother him.

She walks back to the reception desk carrying a new sensation, something like a thrill.

She dials Jerry's extension. It rings eight times. As she waits, it becomes apparent that her heart is beating quickly.

Yello?

Is Jerry there?

You were late this morning, Oscar says.

Train was late, she responds.

Oscar sighs and says that Jerry is out of the office.

Gustave Caron is here, she says. His name is in her mouth for the first time.

You mean Gus? Oscar sounds surprised. He's not due in until next week. Could you tell him that I can't get down there for another hour or so—

He just wanted a room to work in. I don't think he—

Sure, sure. I'll be down to see him when I can.

Oscar hangs up. She hears plastic rattling from the kitchen. The familiar sound of someone struggling to operate the coffee machine.

Standing at the kitchen door, she watches Gustave. He has taken off his jacket. His arms move with uncertainty, skimming over the machine's various buttons.

What is this thrill?

She comes to his side, reaches across him and he stops, his arms suspended. She opens the coffee pod holder and closes it again. After a beat, the machine goes brrzzztttt and spatters dark coffee into the cup below.

Oh. I was too impatient, Gustave says.

The thrill takes a shape as he speaks, his voice low and approving: the thrill is doing things *for him*.

Someone says, alright, mate.

They both turn around. A man from Oscar's team who is wearing green trousers stands there.

Gustave says, Hello, how are you?

Green Trousers scans them both. Slides his hands into his pockets. Good, good. Just settling a few things with the Vivarium account. Difficult bastards, aren't they?

Gustave lets out a short, silent laugh. He is being polite against Green Trousers's over-friendliness. Recognizing this brings her another thrill.

Green Trousers looks at her and nods slowly, as though understanding something. Then he looks back to Gustave and asks if he will be joining them for lunch.

Gustave reveals his watch from beneath his shirtsleeve in a performative motion. I have a lunch meeting with White Stone. I got to London Bridge early, so I am just here to organize some things before I go. If you don't mind.

Sure, sure. No worries, mate. Looking forward to seeing you Monday.

They watch Green Trousers walk away, still nodding to himself, hands tight in his pockets.

Gustave picks up his coffee. Their eyes meet. He raises his eyebrows and gives her a knowing look. Thank you, he says.

I love you, she thinks.

Saturday. Gustave's headshot is there in the blank space before she realizes she is awake.

She is late to meet Jenny at a cafe in Southend High Street; the only cafe in Southend which still just takes cash. Jenny always chooses this place. On the way, she withdraws money from the cashpoint without checking her bank balance.

There is an old couple sitting outside the cafe with a dog. A seagull makes ten noises in a row. The cafe interior is *shabby chic*, mismatched furniture with crochet blankets hung on everything and the smell of cheese toasties. Windows steamed with condensation. The person behind the counter has tattoos. Jenny is talking on the phone when she arrives, waving to her and continuing the phone conversation for two minutes before hanging up. When she sits down the table shunts awkwardly, one leg too short.

They order poached eggs and Prosecco with orange juice.

I try not to buy avocados any more, Jenny says. Do you know how much water it takes to grow just one? Not to mention the pollution caused by exporting them here. Anyway, how are you? Are you still thinking of moving back to London?

Can't afford it yet, she replies.

Why don't you just stay in Southend? It's such a good creative scene now.

She shrugs again.

Have you made any art recently? Jenny asks.

No. You? she responds, knowing the answer.

Jenny clears her throat. Yeah, I've been quite busy. It's so good having a house with a studio now. Makes such a difference. Gareth goes out to work and I just shut myself away all day in the studio. And that little gallery in Leigh is selling my collection now, did I tell you that?

Exciting.

Jenny gives a loud half-laugh. I love how monotone you are, she says. It doesn't even offend me any more.

Plates arrive. Two quivering white bulbs of egg on each. Jenny pierces one decisively. Hot yellow spills out.

Along the seafront, there is a clouded sun and little wind. The tide is out. They walk past flat swirls of mud.

Are you still seeing that guy? Jenny asks.

Which one?

Jenny's exclamative laugh again. Are there really that many?

No. I'm just not sure who you mean.

I mean that guy you were telling me about last time I saw you. God, it was ages ago now. What happened? He sounded alright.

He wasn't interesting.

You're so mean. Jenny turns to one side, brushing hair out of her face. I don't know how you do it.

Do what?

Jenny seems to be picking her words carefully. Like… just casually shagging people. All the time.

All the time?

Jenny looks at her. You know what I mean.

She turns away, squinting at the horizon. Yeah, I *do* know what you mean.

I'm not trying to offend you. Just. I don't understand what it's about. Forget I said anything. I'm just making conversation.

A woman stands on the beach with a toddler stamping the sand around her feet. The woman crouches, raising her palms to still the toddler before undoing the zip of his blue coat. The toddler, unravelled, stumbles from the sand into the mudflats. The woman stands again, long hair swinging.

Leaning back against unwashed pans in the sink, she opens each dating app in turn, pretending to be someone else looking at her profiles. In all of them, the photos are the same. It is obvious they are all selfies, even though she tried taking them to look as though they were taken by someone else. This version of herself on the screen is unsmiling and awkward. Unsmiling and alone. No other people in the frame to suggest she is *sociable* or *popular. Interesting.* Or *successful.* She finds the *deactivate* option for each of the apps.

Are you sure you want to go?

Yes.

Opening the fridge, she is instantly repulsed by its contents, wondering why she has not been repulsed by it before. Tupperware upon Tupperware of pasta in bulk for work. What would Gustave think if he knew that she shovelled spaghetti into her mouth every day? She thinks about shaking her head at herself, at the pasta. To demonstrate to anyone watching that she realizes her mistake. But she decides not to and the image of shaking her head at herself remains only in her mind.

She flicks the fridge door shut again. She googles *what do french men like.*

Travel blogs from American au pairs: *And that's how I began my amazing life in Paris, the most <u>romantic</u> city in the world…* The word *romantic* is hyperlinked. She presses it. Another blog post opens.

Dans Le Sac: How I Met My French Boy (and how <u>You</u> can too!)

The image headlining the article depicts a heterosexual couple standing before the Eiffel Tower, holding hands. The man's back is turned, face hidden. The woman peers back over her shoulder, facing the camera and smiling. Conspiratorial.

Videos on Instagram: long panning shots of Paris. People in stylish clothing. A cafe. *GET READY WITH ME: MY PARISIAN MORNING ROUTINE.* The whispering voice of a young woman. Soft piano music playing. Yoga on bare wooden floors. Skincare. Serum. Products in small white bottles. There she is in the mirror, dressed in monochrome, hair neat but not too neat. Her eyes caught in the sunlight. Beautiful. Great skin. Now she is chopping fruit and putting it into a blender in a marble kitchen. Eating more fruit. A coffee on a balcony, the architecture of Paris spread out before her, Eiffel Tower dominating the horizon. In the next shot the girl loads flowers onto a basket on the front of a bike and then rides the bike through a park. Then she walks a small dog. Then there is a close-up of her hand entwined with a male hand, which wears a heavy and expensive wristwatch.

She thinks of Gustave's big silver watch.

Comments: *so jealous of your life!* crying face emoji crying face emoji

More videos. *HOW I CHANGED MY LIFE AND MOVED TO PARIS. A DAY IN THE LIFE OF A PARISIAN.* Laughter.

A twenty-something girl points to captions as they appear on screen to the rhythm of Europop: *Ten Things That French Guys Find Irresistible.*

Number 3: FLAWLESS SKIN: Time to ditch the make-up! French men like their women effortless and with fresh, clear skin. Not blessed with perfect skin? Time to rethink your skincare routine.

Number 4: LEARN THE LINGO (SLIGHTLY): Did you know that Jane Birkin practised imperfect French? Her charmingly faulty lingo and English accent made her irresistible. So brush up! Mais, not too much.

Jeanne Damas looks into the camera as though it is her mirror reflection and puts on red lipstick.

She watches a Charlotte Gainsbourg interview on YouTube, and wonders whether she should start speaking in hushed tones.

The video freezes. Her phone vibrates, beginning to ring. A video call from Javier. The screen changes to the front camera view, filled by an unflattering low-angle shot of her face. She stares back at herself until Javier eventually hangs up and Charlotte Gainsbourg is back.

She searches:
french girl
french girl style
parisian style
how to look french
how to be a french girl

The images blend. Every *French girl* effortlessly chic and casual. They are all turning, wind in their hair, turning to gaze back at something, someone, red lips opening to show bright white teeth.

The next day she goes out and buys new clothes in *monochrome, classic neutral shades, a pop of colour*. Picking up *a crisp white shirt*, which Ines de la Fressange advised in a *Vogue* interview is *timeless French elegance*, something explodes in her brain and her body fills with light. She buys red lipstick and receives a text from her bank to say her account is nearing its overdraft limit.

Her planned outfit for Monday hangs on the bathroom door frame, footless legs dangling in the dark. The *crisp white shirt*, arms loose.

In bed she stretches out her limbs and closes her eyes. She imagines being elegant and mysterious in a bar. She engages impressively with the anonymous bodies around her, catching the eye of Gustave, who is made curious by her spiky charm. She pushes her hair behind her ear. The vague figures around them blur and disappear.

In the shower the next morning she shaves everything. Moisturizes her entire body. She puts on the *crisp white shirt*. The *tailored black culottes*. The *Converse trainers* – a risk with office dress code, an anxiety she allays with the fact that *Parisians don't play by sartorial rules*. The shirt collar frames her neck elegantly. The material is cold. *French women don't feel the need to expose their cleavage. The appeal is in the mystery, the sensuality.* She adjusts her bra. She sprays perfume behind her ears, then into the air. The white and black feel stark. Noticeable. She is ready to jump over the edge, no longer invisible.

She selects a Charlotte Gainsbourg playlist on Spotify before placing her phone in the bathroom sink: a tip she read somewhere online, something about the shape of the basin enhancing the volume. It does. *How to get that casual, everyday French girl look. That minimal but glowing and oh-so-chic look. French girls don't have time to spend three hours making sure their face is perfect!* She stares. Skin and eye bags grey. Acne scars extra pink. *French women invest in skincare instead of wearing make-up to cover issues.* She applies serums: an exfoliant, niacinamide, vitamin C. Her face glistens with product. She decides to add two layers of her new face cream which cost thirty pounds, pressing it into her skin as she saw on a TikTok tutorial titled *Why French girls never look tired.* She tips her mascara wand, angling it to the roots of her eyelashes for a *naturally lifted* look. She presses red lipstick to her mouth, applies it and then steps back. It is too much. After rubbing it off with a towel, she starts again. Presses on the lipstick. Rubs her lips together. Steps back. At last: *bouche mordue*, the desired look as prescribed to her by Instagram.

There is a banging sound on the wall from her neighbour. Music too loud, obviously. She ignores it, spraying dry shampoo into the roots of her hair, pushing her fingers through it vigorously for extra volume. One rogue curl at the back of her head won't obey. She arranges her hair into the idea of a *messy bun*. It is not messy in the correct way. Her hair is too thin and white patches of scalp appear. She releases sections of hair, pushing her fingers into the roots. Positions her fringe over her eyes. Is this *chic*? She remembers the fifth tip: *The au naturel rule applies to hair, too! French men love carefree locks. Embrace your natural colour. And don't go crazy on the styling tools either – hair should be artfully unkempt.* She regrets dyeing her hair black three months ago. That must be why she always looks so tired. Perhaps she should get *natural, face-lifting highlights.*

With her new hairstyle finally in place, something about her is altered. A sense that this is not her face. It is someone else's. A stranger's. It is not a bad feeling, this sensation of a split inside her, of something breaking apart, because she is filled with light from the inside out. This girl is glowing and, better yet, looks like she does not care.

Her fingers are stained with the colouring of the dry shampoo. Still scrutinizing her reflection, her hands move automatically to turn on the hot tap, to rinse her fingers. The water heats up quickly. Violins become distorted. Then Charlotte Gainsbourg gargles. She looks down. Her phone is under the water. She scalds her fingertips, as she claws at the phone. It twice slips from her hand. Even out of the water, the music sounds as if it is still submerged. She dries the phone hurriedly with a corner of her towel. Maybe it will be fine. Then the music stops. And the screen goes black. She presses the power button. Nothing happens. The phone has died.

—

34

At the office, a man delivers catering boxes and *doffs his cap* at her in an overly friendly manner. She looks away. There is a piece of paper on the top carton. The order sheet. She pulls the lid off the box to check its contents. Croissants. Putting the first box on the desk, she looks inside the one beneath it. More croissants. These are more croissants than she ordered. Her heartbeat quickens. She lifts the lid of the third box. Sandwiches, thankfully. A sensation at the top of her nose like tears forming. The order list confirms everything she remembered ordering. But why are there so many croissants? She calls the catering company.

Thank you for calling City Cooks Limited. Our office hours are nine a.m. to— She hangs up. On a Post-it note stuck to her computer monitor, in her best handwriting, she has underlined *Set up Breakfast by 8:30AM!!*

In the boardroom she arranges fruit in a bowl as a centrepiece. One grape dangles over the edge. She pushes it back, then changes her mind and pulls it back out, deciding that this is an example of *effortless aesthetic*. Like a still-life painting. She starts tessellating the pastries. Gustave will notice her today: for her perfect choice of catering and her eye for artful detail.

When she returns to the reception desk to get the rest of the boxes, Oscar is standing there, smoking a vape. She walks around him wordlessly.

Need any help?

No, she replies without looking at him, feeling unable to speak in more than single syllables. She takes the spare box of croissants into the kitchen and tips it into the bin. There cannot be so many croissants.

In the office bathroom mirror, she adjusts her *messy bun*, pulling out fronds of hair to *frame her face*, then walks quickly across the beige carpet, past the meeting rooms, past the breakfast-filled boardroom, to the reception desk, sitting so heavily that her swivel chair rolls across the floor. She can see three people standing in the boardroom, legs positioned awkwardly around the table, muted chat through the glass. Oscar, Marketing and Green Trousers.

By 09:07, Op-Us have not arrived.

The phone rings. Jerry. Are the guys here yet?

No, she says.

Let me know when the guys are here.

At 09:16 male figures appear through the glass doors and enter reception. Grey Suit, Hadrien and—

Gustave. Gustave is not there.

Oscar appears out of the boardroom, pulling Grey Suit into an enthusiastic hug, slapping him on the back. Voices boom. Grey Suit gestures to Hadrien, who comes forward and shakes Oscar's hand. Jerry clanks down the stairs and joins them, the smallest of them all. The voices get louder. More handshakes. More pats on backs.

They enter the boardroom in formation, shapes in black, grey and blue morphing into one another through the frosted glass. The immaculate hand of Marketing emerges briefly, to gently close the boardroom door. Then the reception becomes silent once more and she feels something close to despair.

She dials the number for the catering company again. Fifteen seconds of a song intro plays on a loop. She waits, her irritation growing. She has to complain. But would a French person call a catering company to make a complaint? The twenty-two YouTube videos she watched about attracting French men advised that she should be more *laid-back*.

Hello, this is—

She hangs up. Logging into her Facebook, she writes: *Hey guys! My phone died (don't ask!). In the unlikely event that you might need me, message me on here.*

She reads it once before editing it.

So my phone died. don't ask lol. message me on here innit.

She sits back. Closes her eyes and opens them. She rereads the post as though she were someone else. Edits it again.

My phone died lol. Message me here.

She visualizes who would *like* the post; someone from senior school, probably, that person who she barely spoke to and yet seems to *like* all of her posts. Or just Jenny. She imagines what Gustave would think if he knew she was lonely. Feeling totally tragic, she deletes it and logs out. No, I'm not lonely, she thinks.

In a brightly lit phone shop close to Fenchurch Street she passes her phone, warm and clammy from her hand, to a shop assistant, while thinking about how the woman's make-up looks *chalky* in the unflattering lighting and that her multicoloured hair is Too Much. Grime music is playing. An advert loops on an LCD screen with clips of young people playing basketball and someone working on a MacBook.

The assistant paws over her phone, pressing the power button.

I've already tried doing that, she says.

Doing what?

Turning it on.

The woman has a badge which says she is an *iPhone Master*. She stares at the phone for a few more moments before saying that, if she were her, she would try taking the phone apart and leaving it in rice overnight.

Right. But I just. I need it to work.

But the chances are, if it doesn't work at all then you will need to buy a new phone. So it makes sense to try your luck and see if you can save this one, doesn't it?

She takes back her phone, a vital but dead stone. So you can't fix it?

We're not a repair shop.

What was the point in me coming here if you're just going to tell me something I could have found out on the internet?

The assistant has a flat expression. I don't know why you came here to get your phone fixed in the first place.

Well, you're my contract provider. Don't you have a duty of care? Can't you just. She raises her free hand then drops it to her side again. I don't know. Give me a phone? Until this one is fixed?

We can't—

Okay. She raises her hands, spinning to leave, already knowing what she said was stupid.

The homeware aisle is at the back of the supermarket in Southend. It is dim and dark, the lighting weirdly low in this area. There are two types of alarm clock on display. The cheapest one is ugly, apparently designed to look retro, but the effect is just tasteless. Oblong face, beige plastic shell. It makes her feel sick. What if she risks no alarm clock, trusting herself to wake up without one. Sleepovers with her childhood best friend always included hours of early-morning loneliness, lying awake on the makeshift bed on the floor while her friend slept. Counting the toys on the shelves – toys which evolved over time – Barbies, hairdressing dolls, plastic babies that soiled themselves. Over time she evolved, too, from lying awake to getting up and going to the living room. One early morning, her friend's father walked in on her in the living room. He was wearing a T-shirt and shorts. Yawning and rubbing his hair. He stopped upon seeing her, saying, Oh. Good morning, and then, What are you reading? There was a newspaper before her on the coffee table. An article about a crisis happening somewhere. She told him. He raised his eyebrows in a manner that suggested he was impressed by her and she felt pleased. The sensation started in her stomach, warm.

She puts the clock back on the shelf and starts to walk away, but then anxiousness overcomes her and she stops. Can she trust her body now? She goes to look for rice, the ugly clock held against her ribs.

Walking to her flat, she passes terraced houses with lights and televisions on. She accidentally meets the eye of a woman smoking a cigarette out of her window, both glancing away quickly.

Back at her flat, she knocks on the door opposite hers. She pulls a polite smile. Fifteen seconds pass. No answer. She knocks again. The door opens. Her smile tightens. Her neighbour appears from half-darkness.

Yes?

Hi. Sorry. What's the time?

The neighbour pulls at the brown cardigan over her shoulders, twists around to look behind her, finding the time displayed somewhere and saying, Ten forty-two. Sensing the neighbour wants to say more, she quickly turns around and lets herself into her flat.

The phone pieces are submerged in rice. She stands by the window in her kitchen area and lights a cigarette. Darkness obscures the view of what in daylight is a bare and untreated patch of land with an empty skip at its centre. She thinks of the woman she saw on the way home from the supermarket, smoking at her window. What is the difference between them? The other woman clearly did not care about her appearance: hair scraped back, fat hanging from her upper arms. In her imagination she fills in the space behind the woman: a littering of plastic toys on the living room floor, television blaring cartoons. She imagines the woman pulling back her hair in the mornings, shouting at her children to get ready for school. They scream and push one another down the stairs. The mother slaps their heads, hassling them to eat sugary cereal, artificial things. Tastes she remembers from her own childhood: white bread and margarine.

The difference between them is obvious. She will never let herself go. And in that moment it feels as though Gustave is beside her, watching her as she smokes a cigarette, looking into the middle distance as though his presence means nothing to her. She thinks about eating fruit in the morning. She thinks about getting a blender. Envisions an apartment with a balcony, with a marble shelf in the bathroom for all her serums. Clean. White. Holding Gustave's hand in a park. Rows and rows of flowers.

She wakes up before the alarm clock. In a square of early-morning light, she unearths phone pieces, blowing residue from them. She reassembles the handset, the power button. Nothing happens. She presses it again. And again, holding it down for longer. She expects to see the start-up screen appear with a flash of reassuring white. But nothing happens. She bashes the phone against the edge of the worktop. She throws it against the wall. It bounces and hits the floor. Lands face down. The screen is still intact. She presses the power button again. Nothing. She straightens her back, rage finding its base. She pulls back her arm and throws the handset hard across the room, watching it hurtle into the bathroom, strike the sink and clatter on the floor.

As she enters through the office door, Jerry's face catches hers. Could you grab a couple of coffees, he says, turning swiftly and not waiting for her to respond.

She loads a pod into the coffee machine, calculates the right number of cups, places them on a tray, then lifts it up and turns slowly. Resets her face to become expressionless. Exhales.

She leans against the boardroom door to push it open.

In front of her, Grey Suit rises up from his seat, blocking her view of the room.

Jerry, did you force this poor girl to make us coffee? We've already got some. He lands a hand on her shoulder, where its weight burns. You idiot. You're an idiot, Jerry, you really are.

Jerry is grinning and saying nothing. Someone is chuckling.

She feels herself being turned back out of the door.

This is a waste, no?

A French accent. Like a rubber band snapping. Her eyes fall on Hadrien. A too-keen smile.

Her focus shifts to the far end of the room. Gustave, leaning back in his chair, fingers resting over his mouth, expression obscured. Did he speak?

Alright. We'll probably need it. Oscar is half-standing, reaching out with his arms. Come on, give us the coffee.

She stalls once more before stepping forward and placing the tray on the table. Cheeks hot. All the bodies in the room watch in silence as she starts handing out the coffees, unable to look at Gustave, the black hole at the other side of the table.

Just leave the tray, someone says.

She stiffens. And in the next moment she finds herself outside of the boardroom. Stopping dumbly, unknowingly, one hand at her mouth. Fingernails meeting teeth. Far away, the reception phone rings.

She leaves the office when the monitor shows 17:29. Outside she squints in the late-afternoon sun. On the other side of the road, a figure emerges from the shade. They are looking down at something in their hands, fingers moving. Close enough now for her to see their military jacket, its light coating of plaster dust.

What are you doing here?

I wanted to see you, Javier responds.

She knows she is frowning. Not at him but at his hands, the skin of his fingers picked sore.

I have been calling you, he says quietly.

My phone isn't working.

Really?

I dropped it. She folds her arms, settling into the half-truth.

Javier looks to the end of the street then back at her. I have one you can borrow, he says.

—

Javier is pulling out his front door keys and explaining how his flatmates are away for the week, cooking at a festival in Portugal or something. She follows him down the hallway to his bedroom. It is smaller than she remembers, thin curtains over the window. Fifties horror movie posters on the wall that she must not have noticed the first time. A skateboard in the corner. MDF furniture. Shelves stuffed with DVDs. A loud thought: who buys DVDs?

He stands before her with a lazy, soft expression on his face. As he links his fingers in hers, it becomes clear that he is attempting to create a feeling of intimacy.

I need a shower, she says.

Okay. He takes a step back. Their arms stretch out between them, like they are about to start dancing. She tries to break away from him but he squeezes his fingers around hers tighter, trying to regain what has been lost. She snatches her fingers out from his hands.

She turns on the shower before undressing. Looking down, she finds a small amount of regrowth around otherwise vaguely neat pubic hair. There is a men's razor resting on the sink. In the shower, she squeezes hair conditioner into her hand, palming it onto the smallest hairs before pulling the razor across them. At the sensation of the blade, she has the realization that Javier would fuck her whether she shaved or not. She wonders how Gustave would want her.

Javier is sitting on his bed, staring down at his hands. When she enters, he looks up and, on cue, she drops the towel, watching his eyes open up for her like wells. She moves to stand in front of him, her hips level with his face. He wraps his hands around her middle, pressing his face into her skin.

I missed you. His voice is muffled.

She processes this with disbelief, letting him pull her sideways. She lands on the bed. He kneels between her legs. She brings an arm over her eyes. Waits. Javier begins running his tongue pointlessly up and down her labia. She sighs loudly. After sixteen seconds he stops, getting her attention by wrapping his fingers around her wrist.

I want to see your face when you come, he says.

She pulls her arm out of his grip and lays it across her stomach. Well, I'm not going to if you keep fucking around. Closing her eyes again, she brings up a presence from the dark: Gustave.

The tip of his tongue has finally touched her clitoris.

Gustave in a suit. Gustave looking at her. Gustave in the boardroom with her. Javier's mouth no longer belongs to him. The motions are not coming from lips, from a tongue, but have become a murmur circling outwards, spreading within her. Gustave's eyes follow her around the room. Gustave appearing in the doorway of the office kitchen. Her hands clench around the duvet of their own accord. Gustave watching her make coffee. She lets out a sound. Javier moans back. Gustave looking at her with the eyes of a predator. Gustave backing her into a corner. The intensity grows, like knocks on a door growing louder. She climaxes. Gasping, Javier pushes himself into her and the sensation runs through her. She keeps her eyes closed. Gustave is back, staring at her from the other end of the boardroom table. Javier gasps again. Pulls out of her quickly. White heat hits her inner thigh.

Sorry, he says.

The phone in her hand loads a background image: a poster matching one on his wall. The time appears. 11:02. Signal and Wi-Fi coverage symbols flicker. Then the phone pings. Pings again. Pings again so rapidly that it interrupts itself.

WE MISS YOU! Do you miss us? Would you come back to us if we gave you a 30% discount for 3 months?

Javier sits down at a table beside the window, rubbing his eyes. She opens Google and searches for Gustave. The same headshots pop up. The strong eyebrows. Dark eyes. The wide nose. That photogenic ease. That smile, so familiar now it is as though he were smiling at her. She skips forward to page eleven, where she finds a photo in which he appears off guard, not smiling, arm over the shoulder of someone sitting at a desk.

Javier's face is now entirely in his hands, bottom lip just visible, a baby pout.

Obligingly, she asks him what is wrong.

He does not respond.

She looks down at the phone again, zooming in on the photo of Gustave off guard. His eyes are focused. What would it be like to become the space he is focusing on?

After seven seconds Javier exhales heavily. Sorry. I have just been having problems with work. This morning I was going to meet with my boss, but he rang me and told me to stay home.

She contemplates what it must be like to be Gustave. He is a force. She cannot be the only one to recognize it.

You're not even listening to me.

I am.

Javier shakes his head and looks away.

Can't you just find another job?

It's not that easy.

Construction sites always need people.

But they don't always want *me*.

Why?

He shrugs. Immigration, he says.

You're from Spain, right?

Colombia.

45

She blinks. I thought you were Spanish.

No. Colombian.

But you told me you lived in Spain?

Yes. But I was born in Colombia. Moved to Spain when my mother died.

Her eyes move around the room as though looking for some kind of support from the furniture.

Javier sniffs and stands up. Forget it. I don't know why I'm even telling you this. He stops in the doorway and she realizes he is speaking to her plainly for the first time. Just be honest with me, he says. Do you even want to be here? Otherwise we are just wasting time.

She stares.

Registering her silence, Javier nods to himself and walks into the hallway.

She raises her voice. You know, you can't miss someone you've met, like, twice. No response. She gets up and finds him in his room, lying on the bed. Did you hear me?

Please, he says. Can we just sleep? His body is turned away from her, facing the wall.

She gets dressed and goes to leave. But she stops in the doorway. Goes over to Javier. His eyes are closed, thick eyelashes curled. She bends over to whisper directly into his ear and says, You're right, I don't want you.

She waits for his reaction. But he pretends to be asleep.

And by the way, she continues, I googled you and I couldn't find anything about you. You must have a really common name.

The next morning the sky is a roof of rain cloud.

Her usual train has been cancelled and the next one is delayed. On the platform people stand still, walk in vague circles, shake their heads, conduct miniature rituals of frustration. She pulls out Javier's old phone and puts it away again, adjusting her bag strap.

When the train finally arrives, there is a rush to board. She sees an empty seat in the middle of the carriage, but two people are already moving towards it from opposite directions. A man and a woman. The woman is nearer. The man picks up his stride. He is large. Propping his rucksack in one arm, he uses his entire mass to barge past her. The woman stumbles, almost falling. The man seats himself and pulls out a book. Clears his throat. Gets comfortable. The woman rearranges herself, looking stunned for a moment. Eventually she finds a handrail and holds onto it, defeated.

A pang. She should say something. She was a witness.

No. *French girls are nonchalant. French girls don't care about the differences between men and women, they're not screaming die-hard feminists with placards. If anything, they simply enjoy these differences. Embrace them.*

In the gaps between passengers, the train windows are visible. Rain spatters hard, violent against the glass. She watches the woman, who stares nowhere.

Motion-activated lights stutter upon her arrival at the office. Green Trousers appears from the bathroom, rubbing wet hands on legs, giving her *the once-over*. We're taking the guys from Op-Us out on Friday, he says. What's the process for booking that?

You just ask me, she replies.

Ask you what?

To arrange it.

I can book it myself. I just wondered how we do it, like do we have to give invoices to Finance? Actually we've got to extend their hotel booking anyway. I'll just go to Finance.

It's. It's better if you just let me do it, she says.

He flaps his hand dismissively. Nah, it's good, he says, before vanishing into the kitchen.

She watches him use the coffee machine. Her fingers open and close, exercising something. Annoyance.

Where are the orange coffee pods?

The what?

The orange coffee pods. Green Trousers pronounces this slowly. The Liberica.

You mean the Arabica.

Liberica.

The orange pod is the Arabica, she says.

The orange pod is the Liberica, he insists.

She drops her bag to the floor and walks to the cupboard beneath the coffee machine. Crouching to open it, out of the corner of her eye she registers the cheap fabric of Green Trousers's green trousers. She pulls out the coffee pod container, rifling through it until she finds an orange pod. She turns it over in her hand to read the label on the bottom: *Liberica*. She brings the pod up slowly and Green Trousers takes it from her upturned palm.

She is sitting at the reception desk when the appearance of Gustave creates a break in time. One moment he's there on the street, the next he is standing before her saying hello.

Hello, she responds. *Casual, airy.*

Oscar and I have a meeting, however I am a little bit early. He is smiling that commercial smile she has seen in his photos. Would you be so kind as to allow me to take up one of your meeting rooms once again?

She brings her hands to her computer keyboard to disguise the tremor in her fingers. And to prolong the interaction by checking the meeting room calendar. The computer has crashed. The tremor has moved to her throat now: the urge to look at him and also the urge to not-look. This is how it feels to be the space that Gustave gazes upon.

Looking up at last, she allows the force of Gustave's eyes to fill her. You weren't here on Monday, she says.

He raises his eyebrows and says, Pardon?

You weren't here on Monday. I ordered some really nice catering.

Oh really? It must have been delicious.

Her insides are red and it must be showing on her skin. It was, she says. It was delicious.

The computer is installing updates. Twelve per cent. Thirteen per cent. Seventeen per cent. Dots spinning. She wants to say everything and nothing at all. Have whatever room you want, she says eventually.

You are spoiling me, he says, and a delicious knife twists. He picks up his laptop bag and walks to the meeting room closest to the reception desk. He leaves the door open. She watches his legs take a seat, pulling himself closer to the desk.

She has the idea to ask him if he would like a coffee. But as she prepares to get up and do so, Gustave stands and appears briefly – on the phone, eyes looking down, already occupied – then closes the door.

She spends over an hour staring at Gustave's disembodied legs and hearing the low rumble of his voice. He must need a cigarette soon. Perhaps if she leaves, he will see her and come to join her. She walks slowly past the room on her way to the entrance. Outside, she lights a cigarette and waits, trying to look *nonchalant*, which is difficult today as the weather is cold and there is a strong wind. Thirteen minutes pass. She lights another cigarette.

The door opens. Her stomach tightens then drops upon seeing it is not Gustave but Marketing.

Oh. I didn't know you smoked, Marketing is saying.

She shrugs.

Marketing is holding a branded reusable coffee cup. I used to smoke when I was at uni, she says. Everyone smokes then, don't they? Now I just vape. But only when I've had a few glasses. I might have a cheeky fag though.

If Gustave came out for a cigarette now, he would see her talking to someone else and gain the impression she is a *talkative* and *popular* person.

She stretches her mouth into what is hopefully a smile but feels like a grimace and says, What did you study?

Marketing looks surprised. Oh, just marketing. And you?

Fine art.

Marketing is nodding slowly. You seem like the type of person who studied art, actually.

She wonders what this means, at the same time knowing exactly what it means. Well. You studied marketing and now you work in marketing.

Ha. Yeah.

The cigarette burns down to the nub. She throws it into the gutter.

But do you still do anything creative? Marketing asks.

No.

How come?

Glancing at the office door, she considers having a third

cigarette, but the prospect of continuing this conversation is off-putting. I don't know, she responds.

Oh. By the way, I left some packages on your desk if you could…

When she returns from the post office, Oscar appears from the boardroom as though having sensed her arrival. Could you make us some coffees? he asks.

Who for?

He is silent for a moment, his expression blank. For the guys, he responds. As she walks past him, Oscar's voice follows over her shoulder, By the way, when anyone from Op-Us comes, you need to put them in the boardroom.

Gustave chose that room, she thinks, breathing in to keep it to herself.

In the office kitchen, on the worktop, a Liberica pod sits half-crumpled in a small pool of coffee. Her lungs inflate. She visualizes herself exploding. How embarrassing that would be. She drops the pod into the pedal bin, wiping over the tiny puddle with a sponge. She walks back to the sink, turns on the tap and holds the sponge beneath the water. Squeezes.

Do you need help?

Gustave. Gustave. Gustave. She glances over her shoulder to confirm it is him. Then glances away just as quickly. The water runs clear through the sponge. In her spine, the sweet dread of Gustave occupying the space behind her.

She opens her mouth and says, No.

Come on, you showed me how to make the coffee. I can at least return the favour. Now, he says, standing at the machine. Which button is it?

Tap off. Sponge down. She is at his side now, reaching across him to switch on the machine. There's four of you, right?

Yes, Gustave replies. Hadrien, he will have a—

I know, she says. Pulls out four porcelain cups. I know what everyone has.

You are an expert, he says. The approval, with the accented drawl of the *r*, pours over her like warm water.

She begins arranging the coffee cups on the tray in a circle, an exercise which she recognizes is pointless as they are empty, but she is unable to do anything else now, needing to have busy hands, not able to concentrate in Gustave's gravitational pull.

He takes one of the cups, disrupting the circle, and places it where it is ready to receive the coffee. His hand returns before her, holding a purple pod by way of a question. She nods, watching how he inserts it into the machine.

The cup fills, and when it is done, Gustave hands her the full cup, which she takes, placing it back on the tray and handing him another empty cup. Their fingertips barely touch, but in the intensity of their closeness it is difficult to believe that they did not.

This dance continues until the circle of coffees is complete. She feels Gustave's eyes bore into the side of her head, his gaze a solid object. She looks at him. Up close he looks different again. Flecks of silver in his black stubble. A mole by his ear. Large earlobes. He says something and there is a delay in her processing what he said.

There is something about you.

What?

The scent of him engulfs her. It's just something about you, he says, voice low. You are so… *intense.*

She blinks. He is close enough now for her to feel his body heat. His eyes search her face, looking to her left eye, her right eye, then her mouth. Examining her.

So. He straightens, slapping a hand on the worktop, gesturing with the other hand to the tray. Voice lifted. Shall we?

Dumb, she obeys, following him towards the boardroom. She knows she is carrying the tray but has no awareness of its weight; likewise, her own body hovers, weightless. Gustave opens the boardroom door for her and she glides in.

Both Hadrien and Green Trousers rise out of their seats to take the tray, guide it to land on the table, faces full of concentration. A spontaneous but smooth operation, as though the tray were an aircraft they were landing. Everyone around the oval table sits and watches, silently bemused.

She searches for Gustave, for a final look, a wordless goodbye. But he is taking his place at the table now and no longer looking at her.

She sits at the reception desk for two hours. Lunchtime comes and goes.

When Gustave emerges from the boardroom, holding a laptop bag, he stops before her. Their eyes attach. Goodbye, he says, smiling.

Her mouth moves with the automatic urge to return his smile. Goodbye, she says.

He stands for a few moments more.

Oscar appears, landing a steering palm on Gustave's back. Come on, stop bothering the ladies, you French bastard.

They leave. The other men filter out of the boardroom, passing before her, but she does not see them. Projected over them is a vision: an estate agent is showing her around a large house in Paris. Sunshine pours through the balcony windows. She wears a long blue dress made of delicate fabric. Shoulders bronzed, she carries a beautiful baby. Her hair is long and sleek, curls calmed. Just right. The estate agent regards her: the young wife. She turns to Gustave, her husband. They converse in French.

The next day, at 14:17, a new email appears in her inbox.

Sender: Gustave Caron. No subject. Something moves inside her.

I find you very interesting.

She closes her inbox and opens theguardian.com. She glances over the words before closing the web browser and opens her inbox again. Pictures Gustave at his laptop, composing the message, finding her name somewhere, perhaps in the deluge of reply-alls. Finding her. Thinking of her. The cursor waits. She tries to write a reply, fingers rising to the keyboard but giving nothing. Deciding not to reply immediately, she spends fourteen minutes realigning the office kitchenware and then exits the building to march around the block twice. Resolves in her walking that she will not tell Gustave anything about herself. What is there to tell him, anyway? He already recognizes something in her, without knowing anything about her. How completing it feels, the attention of a mature Frenchman.

She returns to the desk and types.

Is that so?

Deletes. Types.

What do you find interesting about me?

Deletes. Types *Is that so?* again, which on reflection is open-ended enough to not seem too keen. She presses Send, then sits on her hands. She thinks about pretending to read the *Guardian* again. The reception phone rings and she ignores it. Three minutes later, Gustave replies.

Tomorrow is my last day in London. Perhaps you have some time for me? I would like to get to know you…;)

Her adrenaline stalls. A brief crest of embarrassment. The winking face. Based on the minimal personal information she's gleaned online, Gustave must be in his mid forties. She has not imagined him ever using emojis. A sensation she recognizes as *the ick*. The reception suddenly feels small, shrinking in around her, the windows closing in. The sky outside threatens to downpour. She swallows the ick, resolving not to think about his use of emojis any more. Tomorrow is his last day.

Did you get a call from something-something? Jerry's ankles at the top of the stairs.

Sorry?

Something-something.

She squints. Jerry is saying the name of a company, some thrown-together composite of several words.

I'm waiting for a call from them, he says. It's urgent. Make sure you answer the phone. The ankles vanish.

Gustave's email signature is a weird marker. *GUSTAVE CARON – EUROPEAN SALES DIRECTOR – OP-US. OPERATION US! TOGETHER. TOP TIP: If something sounds too good to be true... there's probably a scammer behind it.*

The phone rings and she answers it. Hello, Datata. Sorry, where are you calling from? Where? Which— Okay. She transfers the call to Jerry and puts down the phone.

Into the email, she types *Here's my number* and presses Send. Deep inhale.

Gustave responds, saying, *Cool. I will text you. ;)*.

She gets up. The artificial plant still has a layer of water between its pebbles. She pours in more and the water runs down the side of the pot, turning the carpet dark.

—

When the rain begins it is slow, heavy. Two people move side by side past her, forcing her onto the kerb. She tuts. Her phone makes a notification sound and she feels briefly elated. But it is a message from Jenny, not Gustave, and the elation ends.

Sorry running late!!!!

An instant regret: she should have asked Gustave for his number, instead of handing hers over, unprompted. Or even delayed giving it to him. *The Parisian woman is not desperate. She makes him wait.* Now the power is his.

There is a sparse crowd on the pavement outside the art gallery. People standing in groups, in threes, in couples. Cheap beers. Haircuts. Oversized clothes. She remembers what she hates about artists: they look stupid on purpose. But no one in the crowd is on their own and they are all younger than her. If only Gustave were here. If only he knew she was at an opening, just checking out some contemporary art. There are some things she wants him to know about her. But for these things to be true she needs him to think it for himself: that she is *cultured, interesting*. If only he would message her now, then she could tell him, *casually* and *nonchalant*, I'm just at an art gallery. She has a rich life outside of him. *French girls do not depend on their man.*

Inside the gallery there is a table with bottles of beer and a small tin with a paper sign saying *Pay What U Feel*. The place is busy. The paintings on the wall are brightly coloured and crudely evoke images of men in bunny ears and latex. Objectively bad, she thinks, moving on to a large photograph of someone's legs in a bath, bush of pubic hair at the top like a head. The photo is dark enough for her to see her reflection in the glass. She conjures the presence of Gustave filling in the space next to her. If he texted her now, she could impress him with her critique of the work. And she would tell him that she is here with a friend, who is not running late, and that she is not here on her own. Then again, would he find it *more interesting* if she attended galleries on her own? Is this something French girls do? She is about to take out her phone and google this when there is the sound of glass being rapped upon repeatedly. The chattering of the crowd stops, all bodies turning towards the back of the building where two girls are standing on a podium, both in black military clothing.

Ladies and gentlemen, one says.

The women begin speaking one after the other, voices raised.

Ladies.

Gentlemen.

Ladies.

When did you get laid?

She checks her phone. No messages.

Gentlemen.

Were you gentle?

Ladies.

Did you come?

She gets the point: base-level feminism. Bored, she looks around. There are some people scratching their chins. Others looking at the floor. The gallery walls are higher than she realized. She looks up and finds an artwork hung from the rafters. Her eyes adjust, the design clarifying. *THE FEMININE MYSTIQUE WILL KILL YOU.*

Someone from the crowd is looking at her. A man, who gives a soft smile.

She mouths, What?

Embarrassed, he looks towards the performance again. Fuck this, she says out loud, pushing through the crowd with everyone's eyes on her.

—

On the train, the phone battery is at twelve per cent. She sits and holds it before her, wondering if she can change the phone background. Do French girls personalize their phones? It vibrates in her hand. The inner ohmygodohmygodohmygodohmygod ends abruptly when she sees the message is from Jenny.

Where are you??

She closes the notification. The disappointment is ruinous. She decides that when her phone vibrates again, she will simply not look at it immediately. Reminds herself: *French girls are not dependent on the attention of men.*

On Pinterest she searches *what french girls wear on dates.* Images of long-limbed women walking down a street, tucking their hair behind one ear. The images are gratifying somehow. Comforting. She will be one of them soon. Her thumb strokes the images up and up and up, scrolling continuously and opening tabs, awaiting something, anything, from Gustave, until the phone dies. She pokes her tongue into her cavity. Bites at a hangnail, which peels off to leave new, pink skin. It is fine, she thinks. When she gets home, she will charge the phone and find a message from Gustave. And she will pretend she did not see it immediately because her phone battery just happened to run out, oopsie! All because she is *laissez-faire* and does not depend on her phone. Gustave will be sitting and worrying, wishing that he had messaged her sooner. Perhaps he has missed his chance.

Gustave takes the standard white walls and fake beech laminate flooring of her flat as *minimalism*. He embraces her at the window, holding her there. She can feel his arms around her middle. They make love wordlessly, knowing that they are making love, because they are lovers – something special and more European. Afterwards they lie naked, her head on his chest, while he strokes her hair. She feels the humidity of his skin against her ear.

I want to know about your childhood, she says.

When he replies, the sound comes from his chest. What do you want to know?

The scene of them on the bed, folded over each other, pauses. She restarts the conversation. An extra moment to get reacquainted with the sensation of Gustave against her.

I want to know about your mother, she says.

What do you want to know?

What was she like?

For five seconds Gustave says nothing, still running his fingers through her hair. Then he stops. When she turns her head up to see his face, his eyes are watery. You know, you are like her in a lot of ways, he says.

She stops the fantasy, wondering if this is Too Much.

It is Friday. She speeds through the Essex countryside in her new black-only uniform. *Simplicity is key.* Yesterday's rain has cleared the skies. A blue-sky morning. A pheasant appears and disappears. She closes her eyes, feeling warmth through the glass, thinking about how she will always call him Gustave and never Gus. Gus is an ugly name. Gustave, however, is not. And every time he is referred to by his full name he will think of her. She calls me that, he will tell his colleagues, a small smile on his face, knowing he belongs to her. And they will imagine her so *chic* and *monochrome* and *challenging*.

Oscar approaches her as she walks to the reception desk and says, You look like you're going to a funeral.

The comment hangs in the air, awaiting a response. Today she feels light, fluid and capable of talking.

Aren't you meeting with Op-Us tonight?

He blinks. Yes.

Where are you meeting them?

Oscar looks at his phone and brings it to his ear, appearing to start a conversation as he wanders away and disappears up the stairs.

She checks her own phone, knowing it has not vibrated, and yet. No messages from Gustave. She rereads their email exchange, running the words over and over. The taste of them. They were written for her. It is soothing. Even the winkies have lost their initial repulsiveness. She decides to find them charming, maybe tease Gustave for it. In the future they will have a late-night conversation about the initial stages of their relationship. She will reveal that the winky faces repulsed her, and nearly put her off him entirely. And they will laugh. She will mention it in her bridal speech at their wedding. Everyone will laugh and laugh.

Five hours and forty-seven minutes later. No messages. The bin under her desk contains several empty biscuit packets. On her desk there are packages waiting to be taken to the post office. Her body is fixed, waiting. Tension at the base of her neck. Perhaps he is just so busy. She understands and he will love her because she understands that he is just so busy and she is so *patient* and *caring*. It hurts, though.

18:18. She is hanging around beyond her usual 17:30 finishing time. Nobody seems to notice this as they leave the office. She has a headache. Again she is picking apart her email exchange with Gustave. His final email: *Cool. I will text you.* Perhaps she read it wrong? Nothing to cling on to here apart from the supposed promise that he will text her. She read it as casual, not monosyllabic, which is becoming ever clearer now as the words separate, vast with nothing between them. Maybe he was put off already. She gave up her phone number at the earliest opportunity and it repulsed him. Why would he lie about texting her, then? Well, what else would he say? He had to be polite. He is a gentleman. Just because he prefers women who are mysterious and chic and subtle and not overeager and desperate like her, he knows that this does not warrant treating her with contempt. God, he really is perfect. *French men are true appreciators of the woman – her sensuality, her appeal, her allure.* She feels like crying.

Oscar and Green Trousers descend the stairs. Green Trousers is wearing brown trousers. They are talking between themselves, making to leave. She watches them move past the window, up the street. She waits ten seconds, then grabs her bag, and on her way out of the door runs into Marketing.

Oh, your red lipstick looks nice.

She ignores Marketing and tries to leave before her.

But Marketing is talking again. Hey, I just wanted to say thank you for sending those packages out for me today.

She glances up the road. Oscar and Green Trousers have vanished. It's fine, she responds quickly.

Honestly, you're such a big help—

It's literally my job. I'm the receptionist. I have nothing else to do.

Marketing stops talking, her face changing. Okay, she says.

Something else needs to be said. She examines Marketing's face: winged eyeliner, too-thick contour, pink lip gloss. This is satisfaction enough. She turns and leaves the office, Marketing behind her, forever basic. Travels quickly up the street, until it separates in two directions. Seeing a brown leg disappearing around a corner, she walks faster, following Oscar and Green Trousers beneath a huge railway arch, trains from London Bridge screeching above. She stops, watching the two men enter the quiet road ahead, entering a bar on the left, its entrance framed with ornamental trees. On the right there is a grotty pub, a crowd of people outside, smoking and vaping and drinking. She moves towards the crowd, edging into them. Lights a cigarette. Surreptitiously positions herself to see into the comparatively high-end bar opposite. Its windows are slightly tinted, making it difficult to—

There he is. Gustave. Standing and bear-hugging *the guys*.

She drops her cigarette. She resolves to be patient. I will wait here, she thinks, lighting another cigarette. If this relationship is going to work, she must give Gustave the space to have his fun and do what he needs to do. To be understanding. The woman he comes home to. *The Parisian woman is equally as laissez-faire when it comes to matters of the heart. She does not chase a man – instead she sits back, assured that he will come to her.*

She drinks red wine and searches *the feminine mystique* in Google, but the resulting text is difficult to read because she is unable to think. She recognizes that she should be hungry by now; in fact she is hungry, or she should at least eat.

Two hours pass. The light outside changes, becoming dark blue. People glance at her, intrigued or disgusted to see a young woman drinking on her own. She ignores them, drinks more wine. Glances over to the bar as casually as possible. She blinks. Then Gustave is gone. Inward panic. Perhaps he went to the bathroom or something. She checks her phone. No messages. She reaches into her bag for her cigarettes, but the packet is empty. The rest of *the guys* are getting up from the table now, walking slowly out of view. She folds her arms around herself. She waits to see if they trickle out onto the pavement. They do not. New people take over their table.

What to do now. She walks in one direction for a few paces, stops, then turns the other way. She has to stay in London, to be ready for Gustave if he texts her. When. When he texts her. Going home would mean to die.

She wanders around the area for thirty-five minutes. Ducks into Borough Market and ducks out just as quickly. She sees Gustave everywhere. She repeats his text over and over: *Cool. I will text you. Cool. I will text you.* A thought she has been trying to hold back returns: she is Too Much. Too eager, too desperate. And now she has repulsed him. She stops looking at windows, feeling ugly.

She comes to the small park where she usually eats lunch. It is empty in the dark. She paces to the end, slows, sits on a bench. The phone is still in her hand, rounded corners pressing against her stomach. She wills it to vibrate. The time says 23:35. It is late. It is too late. Cold night air seeps through her clothes, fills her skin, settling in her bones. A person enters the park, glances at her, glances again, then keeps walking. No one can know she is being rejected by Gustave. Perhaps she should have kept her options open. *They enjoy the attention of multiple admirers at once. For French girls, 'dating' is as much philosophical as it is sexual.* She pushes her chin downwards into herself, becoming small, wanting to not be philosophical or sexual, not wanting to be anything. Black leaves hiss on black trees. An unknown amount of time passes.

She initially does not believe the sudden throb in her hand and pretends not to notice. But the urge to look is overwhelming. She counts to ten. Then another ten. Thirty. Before the minute is up, she peeks down, turning the phone ever so slightly to see its screen lit up in the crook in her elbow.

Guess who. ;)

She takes out a make-up bag. Using the light of her phone, she opens a pocket mirror to find a cold face staring back at her, flared up, almost purple. She rubs her lips together until they grow pink with blood. She presses a matte powder onto her face, layering over the pockmarks. She blends at the edges, angling back her head to inspect. Eyes looking wet, face looking waxy. She uses a small spiral brush to comb her eyebrows, a pencil to fill in the gaps. With the mascara she angles the tip to make it appear like she is not wearing mascara at all. Presses more red lipstick to her lips – just enough, just kissed. Finally she rolls a liquid eyeliner bottle around in her fingers, considering whether this would be too much. Too Much, she decides, dropping it back into the make-up bag. A new layer of make-up over her existing make-up. She sprays perfume three times in the space above her head. It falls, a light rain. She checks her phone. Seven minutes have passed. She waits three minutes more to achieve a reasonable amount of time for someone who is *laissez-faire* but also curious to know the identity of the person who has sent her an anonymous message.

Give me a clue? she writes.

Gustave responds two minutes later with a Google Maps address. A hotel. *Why don't you come here and find out?*

The hotel is only four streets away. She walks slowly. Spotting its sign lit up, she slows more, then stops completely. She reaches down to brush some fluff from her left thigh, imagining how someone might see her from a distance, how they will notice her outfit. The difference is in the detail. *From the office to the cocktail bar. From day to night.*

The purple mood lighting of the hotel interior is too stimulating. She can hear music – possibly *soft jazz*. There is someone standing behind the front counter, hotel staff, eyes down and ignoring her.

And to the right of the lobby, in her peripheral vision: Gustave. His skin lit purple. Big dark eyes, bigger and darker. His feet on a threshold where marble meets carpet. The edge of her old life, ending, crossing into the new. She panics briefly and then swallows it.

Gustave presses the button for the lift while she practises her face, preparing for him to look at her again. They stand side by side before the lift door, their bodies distorted, merging in the brushed metal. Addressing his blurred mirror self, she finds she is able to speak. How was your evening? she asks.

Oh, you know, he responds, hands in his pockets. The smudge of his mouth moves almost imperceptibly.

Yes, she thinks sagely. Yes, I do know.

The lift doors part. Gustave presses the button for the seventh floor and the doors close on them. As they travel upwards, she feels him turn to her. His mouth is tipped up at one side. An ambiguous expression. Then he looks away again, clearing his throat. It feels as though she has done something wrong.

The hotel room smells like what she thinks is sandalwood. A large rose-bronze analogue clock on the wall says it is past one o'clock. The walls are grey. Gustave's suit jacket is cast on the white bedspread like an oil spill. She stands by the door, watching his movements. He paces around the bed to the other side of the room, parting a crushed velvet curtain and opening a floor-to-ceiling window with railings preventing guests from walking out into the air. He pulls out a cigarette packet from his shirt pocket and lights one. Then he glances at her in a way that suggests he is unaffected by her presence. She is not forgotten – just there. Make yourself comfortable, he says, gesturing vaguely.

Something about the situation is off. As though a different Gustave texted her and brought her here. What does he expect her to do, standing here with the bed between them. Her eyes catch on a blue patch on the ceiling, a plastic bag tied around the smoke alarm. The cheapness of this is strange, scuffing the atmosphere.

She puts down her bag, tucks hair behind her ear. Wanders around the room for a bit, trying to look thoughtful and interested. Not looking at him, letting him look at her. The room is large. There is a closed door which must be the en suite. She opens it and peeks in. Oh, nice, she says, too brightly, closing the door again. She nears a table, picks up something, puts it down. Gustave, as she had hoped, is watching her.

Can I have one?

Of course.

He lights her cigarette with a concentrated expression, leaning towards her, looming close. From the bright windows hanging in the darkness outside, she wonders how they might look standing here together, smoking. There are a few grey hairs visible on his chest. In the office they were so connected. She thinks about how to bring them back to this, what to say. Something cool, offbeat and flirtatious.

Tell me something about you, she says.

Gustave's face does not change. He taps ash onto the carpet. What would you like to know?

Something surprising.

But you don't know me, he says. Everything could be a surprise.

She wets her lips in preparation for the next line, feeling herself take on the emboldened, seductive character she always imagined herself to be. Then surprise me, Gustave.

He blinks at her. With a final drag, he flicks the cigarette out of the window, over the railings, and returns both hands to his pockets. Okay, first of all. Call me Gus. Please.

Her voice wobbles once. Why?

Gustave. It's an old name. It was my... the father of my grandfather? Great-grandfather, no?

She taps her cigarette, although there is no ash on it. Don't you like it?

Well, I never met him. There's no. No attachment for me. So it's just an old man's name. And anyway, you're pronouncing it wrong. It's *Gustave*. Just call me Gus.

She looks out of the window. If she is to bring him up in conversation as Gus – my boyfriend Gus, my husband Gus – how are people supposed to know he's French? She will have to compensate by dropping the fact in. My husband Gus, who is French. My French husband, Gus. My husband, who is from France. From Paris. Have you met my husband, Gus? He's Parisian…

This situation is becoming complicated. Without checking how much of her cigarette is left, she casts it out of the window, watching the lit end travel down, down, down. Tell me something else, she says.

Alright. Gustave straightens. Well. I'm from Paris.

I know. Her mouth hangs open after this has escaped.

You *know?*

Well, yeah. I mean. Look at you.

His face looks like the headshots she found online. That jaw-set smile. It makes her feel strange.

Your turn, he says. Tell me about yourself.

Southend is beating at her larynx, fighting to escape her mouth. The two McDonald's. The beach with stones that hurt your feet. The street she grew up on with the halfway house next door. The litter. The kitsch. The smell, oh the smell. The noise at night. The vomit on the pavement. To reveal this would be to reveal herself completely.

But how he surveys her. His eyes are black. She has a new life to fill. She reaches out, hand falling upon something, his fingers, enclosing, pulling herself towards him, watching his face coming closer, closer, his eyes registering her nearness, the up-close pixelation of his skin. She does not close her eyes, not wanting to. By the nearness of his face she knows her lips are on his. At first she cannot feel it, so she keeps pushing, pushing, finding him. It should feel euphoric by now, like crossing a frontier. And then the taste of him comes. Tobacco and alcohol. She reaches with her tongue for his tongue. Drawing away, his eyes are the first thing she sees again. And an awareness that her own face is fixed, ready for his gaze. His attention: she needed it and now here it is.

Gustave is bringing her back, kissing her again. The sensation of being held underwater. Not breathing. Now breathing, into him. He responds, breathing back. The sound of the sea. Tongue, teeth. At first it feels like she is travelling of her own accord, feet finding the way, until she understands that Gustave's hands are around her, guiding her body towards the bed. How he is holding her now will stay with her forever. How he is laying her down on the bed, bringing her head to the pillow. Face full of concentration, concentration on her. Only on her. She brings her hands around and over his neck, feeling stubble with her thumb. Thinking only: I want. I want. I want. Gustave places a finger under her chin. Tips her face up to meet his. The sensation of a match striking in her stomach, becoming aflame. A gasp escapes her, back arching, opening up to him, her body pooling like liquid. Where are his hands going now? Her skin tingles at a high frequency, almost numb. Parting her legs, she draws them around him. The full weight of him against her, pressing her into the bed, sinking.

The hotel room door disappears.

Once your Frenchman kisses you, that's it! You are officially a couple. Congrats!

His head snaps back, mouth away from hers. He has a new expression: blank, mouth loose, slack. The change in his face is a signal. She brings her hand to his face, pulls him back to her. Pressing lips against his. At first his mouth softens and the warmth returns. She pushes herself into him. But then his mouth closes, rejecting her. Leaving her body open as he climbs off her. Cold air filling the space where he was.

The surface of the bed moves with his shifting weight. She stiffens against the wave.

He sits on the edge of the bed with his back to her, his shoulders up, hands rubbing his face. Flash of that expensive wristwatch. She reaches out, fingertips grazing his shirt. That is cold too. He does not respond, does not look at her. Everything inside her is sinking.

I'm sorry, he says eventually.

Why? she blurts out, flinching at herself. Why text her? Why bring her to the hotel? What else happens here? Doesn't he know that she would give herself to him? That this is what she is here for.

He lies down on the bed.

The night has been kicked away. She was too eager, too desperate. Too Much. Did he see her waiting for him outside the bar? Wandering around London Bridge? Was he watching her, sitting in the park waiting for his text, getting cold and sad? It feels like he's always watching her, wherever she is.

He is on his phone now, fingers moving fast. What will he say about her, this night, to his friends: a mistake, a regret? She decides to leave. This will show him she's not desperate and has other places to be. She pushes herself up. Her feet dig into the deep pile carpet, which opens up and drops off, an oceanic trench.

His voice comes from behind her, You are upset?

She feels his eyes on her back.

No. She turns, reeling in her desperation. Should I leave?

Now she has asked his permission, the situation is worse. There are no more trains home.

I have an early flight tomorrow.

She stays where she is.

We should sleep.

The bed is moving again. She watches Gustave stand, remove his wristwatch with a look of concentration and place it on the bedside table, along with his phone. He undresses, down to his boxer shorts, and gets back into the bed. All the lights are on. She is still standing in the middle of the room.

Stay.

The trench closes back up. It is an effort not to rush straight to him. She undresses down to her underwear and slides into bed beside him. Gustave turns off the lights. Another period of silence which threatens to be never-ending. Is he pretending to sleep? She decides to count to ten in her head before moving closer to him. Then, leaning on one arm, she examines the curve of his ear: a flashback to Javier. Another guy pretending to sleep. What is it about her that makes men think the only way to escape her is to be unconscious? Is she that powerful? Or that annoying?

Gustave turns around. They stare. She is self-conscious about him seeing her face from a low angle. Hi, he says.

They are kissing again and it feels like being dragged underwater. She is grasping and grabbing at him. The duvet is gone. He is pressing himself against her then pulling back. His skin is cool, strangely smooth. Now she is on top of him. Mouths together again and again and again. Her eyes closed. She hears herself saying into the darkness: I like everything about you.

And then his mouth closes a second time. Stop. It is getting late.

The dismay. She is hot. She tries reaching down into his shorts. He laughs, moving her wrist away. Holding it aloft. When he gradually lowers her hand it feels as though her arm will snap. He gives it back, pressing it to her middle. She is in shock, still, as he rolls out from under her, turning away from her onto his side and saying firmly, *Bon nuit.*

She does not sleep. Sitting up in bed, she turns on the television. Mutes the sound immediately to avoid waking him. A small clock at the corner of the screen says it is just gone 02:00. She flicks through the channels and leaves it on a twenty-four-hour news programme. She watches awhile, her eyes unfixed. The numbers on the clock move slowly. Sometimes they seem to stop altogether. She looks to the ceiling instead, traces the coving, instinctively hugging her arms around her half-naked body.

Across the room the curtains are still parted, the window wide open. But there is no air in here. She will never sleep, she thinks. She feels sick. Or hungry. She reads the same headlines scrolling across the bottom of the screen over and over, the words suggesting nothing. When Gustave moves, she turns to watch, readjusts the duvet if it starts to fall off him. She is taking care of him, she thinks. She will be awake when he awakes. She will not make any more mistakes.

Through the open window the sky is clear and bright, and when she turns over there is no one on the other side of the bed. Everything is lopsided and wrong. Rubbing the backs of her hands against her face, to erase any mess of her accidental sleep, she says his name out loud. It hangs in the air, unanswered. She sits up. His jacket is gone, his laptop bag. It takes her a moment or two to notice there is a note with the hotel logo on the table beside her.

Get room service. Datata are paying for it. ;)

He even drew the winky face. Gustave is gone and he is laughing at her. Surely not. She crumples the note and drops it onto the carpet. It is not right. It is not real. The room is so big and bright. And she is here by herself. And that is that. Surely not. Surely this is not the end.

What now? Do as he says. She picks up the hotel phone to call room service. Twenty minutes later, what she has ordered arrives. Coffee. Orange juice. Croissants, jam, butter. Fruit. Champagne. Her mind is blank. As she eats, she tastes nothing. A flash of pain from her rotten back tooth. But she eats and drinks through it, because she fell asleep and he left. She must have been so ugly when she slept. When he looked at her as she slept. She will never trust her body again.

She leaves the hotel. The streets are empty, no flow of bodies to batter her as she makes her way to Fenchurch Street. Her reflection flashes in office windows, shops, restaurants. She is seeing herself everywhere and from all angles, hair somehow moving in *carefree waves*. She could easily be in an Instagram photo with the hashtag *frenchgirlchic*. But then she does not have Gustave and without him the image is incomplete. Pigeons scatter.

On the train she considers googling *should i text him first*. A sudden thought stops her fingers mid-motion. Gustave is not the type of person to check Google for answers on how to do things. Therefore she is not this type of person either. Outside the window, scenery begins to pass fast, faster. Grey and metal to brown, brown, brown. Blurring. Her mind turns in on itself, back through the answers she already knows. *Yes, go for it. No, wait three days. Always respond. Leave him on read for one day. Some men see it as a turn-on. Some men prefer to be chivalrous and take the lead. How to get him interested in just one text. The rules of texting as explained by guys. The rules of texting as explained by a seasoned hoe.* But in the end all that she has is the memory of Gustave, the press of his weight on her. Green fills the windows. They are both travelling through time but in different directions. Part of her has gone with him.

In her flat, in the kitchen, cigarette in her mouth, she makes coffee, pouring boiled water in a circular motion into the cafetiere, the way several recipe blogs had advised her: to get the full flavour of the bean. She imagines Gustave seeing her, thinking that she looks like a French actress from the sixties. So why is she not with him? But then what did she expect – to go with him to Paris today? Idiot. Idiot. How desperate of her. She will have to learn to wait.

She stands her phone against a set of bowls on a shelf, high enough to look as though someone else is taking the photos, and takes thirty-one photos of herself from angles which capture the essential details: between shutter sounds mussing up her hair or sweeping it casually back, and her outfit, and the fact she is making coffee and smoking a cigarette.

Scrolling through the camera roll, she chooses a photo: just enough of her face to show that she is attractive, but not enough to dilute her mystique. She changes all her profile pictures to this one: Instagram, WhatsApp, TikTok, Facebook, Gmail.

On Duolingo she matches flashcards without thinking, her memory of GCSE French returning faster than she'd imagined, speeding her through several levels. An image of her and Gustave outside a cafe in Paris, speaking quickly in French. The Duolingo owl congratulates her for something and she becomes aware of stiffness in her neck, bent from staring at her phone. *What keeps the French girl so interesting and appealing to her lover? She has a life of her own! You will not find her sitting at home scrolling on her phone, waiting around for him. Mais non! The French girl is out rubbing shoulders in the hottest spots in town. Perhaps she is telling bawdy jokes and philosophizing at an elegant dinner party. Or perhaps she is with her other lover in another city...*

She messages Jenny, asks what she is doing.

After forty-seven minutes, Jenny responds: *Just out for some drinks. X*

She analyses the message. The full stop. The single X. The lack of invitation.

She enters what she would describe as a *mid-tier* cocktail bar, patronized mainly by city boys with matching haircuts doing coke. She is on her tiptoes at the bar, looking for the flash of Jenny's dyed hair in the crowd. She catches the eyes of a woman who is beautiful in an elevated way, sitting opposite a city boy. There is an understanding between them: what it is to be beautiful in such a way and therefore too good for the world they find themselves in. As the woman turns away, the change in light discloses her heavily highlighted and contoured face, lip fillers. It is too late for her. She leaves the bar and heads to the next place Jenny might be.

The smell of bleach and stale beer. Gustave would never come here. She will never come here again.

Someone calls her name. Jenny's boyfriend is standing at the bar, waving to her. And there is Jenny, sitting at a table. She walks over.

Jenny registers her, staring. Oh. Hello.

Hello, she says back, sitting down.

Jenny's boyfriend comes over and presses a finger to her shoulder, asking what she wants to drink. She asks for a red wine. Then she and Jenny sit in silence. She pretends not to feel awkward, deciding that she is taking ownership of the situation by doing this. She is just hanging out with friends like Gustave would imagine her doing. Not thinking about him or depending on him at all. She almost begins whistling. She wonders if Jenny notices that there is something different about her; that she is suddenly effortless and beautiful.

Jenny, playing with her empty glass, asks, What happened the other night?

What do you mean?

You didn't wait for me at the opening.

You were late.

That's why I asked you to wait. But you just left without saying anything.

My phone died.

The words come easily, almost conversationally, deflecting Jenny's upset with ease.

Jenny's boyfriend returns, holding two drinks. Two other men are with him. One is conventionally attractive. Dark hair. Strong sharp cheekbones. White teeth. The other one is not attractive. The men sit down and spit a conversation around the table, something crude. She watches Jenny over the top of her wine glass. Jenny has her head in her hand and a downturned expression. Jenny is moody and not fun. In comparison, she is fun and attractive.

Tuning into the conversation, she says the most relevant thing that comes to mind. It is funny. The unattractive one laughs. The attractive one bites, as she predicted he would. She says something back. The unattractive one laughs again, so keen to please her. The attractive one negates her again. She turns to the unattractive one, appealing for backup. He complies. Jenny's boyfriend also says something. The attractive one, not looking at her now, says something vaguely insulting about the unattractive one. Jenny's boyfriend laughs loudly. The unattractive one looks momentarily embarrassed, eyes flicking to her for support.

Jenny pushes back her chair noisily and walks towards the toilets, and they all turn to watch.

She lifts and drains her glass, replacing it on the table too heavily, and announces that she needs a cigarette, has anyone got one?

I do, says the attractive one.

Outside, the attractive one is lighting her cigarette for her. The fit of his jacket and the style of his shoes suggests that he might have at least read a few books. She pictures Gustave seeing her now, independent and getting on with her life, his desire for her growing, becoming jealous of the attention she is receiving from this attractive stranger, who is asking how she knows Jenny.

We went to college together, she answers. Noticing her cigarette has gone out, she gestures for his lighter. He obliges. The unattractive one has followed them out, eyes zoning in on them alternately, trying to join the conversation.

The attractive one tells her that she doesn't look like she's from Southend. The unattractive one initially snorts, then mocks the attractive one by saying, You're not from round 'ere are you, with an accent like a hostile villager. She looks to the floor and blows out smoke, knowing she appears extremely cool at this moment. The unattractive one changes tack, really looking at her. Actually yeah, he says. You look, like, Polish or something.

She looks different by virtue of Gustave's attention. But to mention her French lover at this point would change the dynamic of the evening. Both men will turn their attention elsewhere.

I live in Paris, she says.

The unattractive one asks if she's French.

Oui, she says.

Inside, she squeezes into the gap beside Jenny at the bar.

I'm pissed off at you, Jenny says.

Why?

Because you just disappeared the other day without saying anything.

I told you. My phone died.

Why didn't you wait for me?

The art was bad.

Jenny attempts to catch the eye of one of the bar staff. They ignore her.

You and Waheed seem to be getting on well, Jenny says.

Who?

Waheed. The bloke you just went for a smoke with. He's engaged, you know.

Another conversation. Everyone has to lean in to hear each other. This time she says something that makes Jenny's boyfriend belly-laugh. The attractive one puts a hand on her arm to make a point.

On the table behind them is a woman she has found herself looking at twice. She recognized her nose first. A girl from her sixth-form college who dropped out after the first year.

The unattractive one is vying for her attention, asking if she can speak French *now*, just say something in French. She ignores him and gets up. Bathroom, she says out loud, thinking that someone has asked where she is going.

—

In the cubicle she checks her phone – no messages – and thinks, That's fine, that's fine. She is too busy to check her phone anyway. On her way out she bumps into the attractive one, who says, Don't worry, I'm not following you in, to which she replies: Wish you were. Then she finds herself at the bar, standing behind people waiting to be served. Adrift. Where is Gustave and what is he doing. Is he thinking of her.

Within a minute the unattractive one is standing beside her. He smells like beer and cannot hold his drink. Are you going to give me some French lessons then?

Shut up, she says.

He persists. It's really sexy that you're French. Don't know what it is. Sorry, is that too much? The attractive one joins them and the unattractive one tries appealing to him, You agree, right? It's really hot that she's French, so hot, come on just say one word, one word in French, anything.

Alright mate, the attractive one says, using the opportunity to show he's above this sort of thing, and simultaneously to save her, she thinks. She takes his arm, pulling him out to the smoking area.

He lights her cigarette again and stares at her with a small smile. His eyelids lower and she watches as his face comes closer. His eyes close. Expectant. Then his mouth presses against hers.

Jenny told me you're engaged, she says.

He withdraws quickly, smile gone. Clears his throat. Right. Okay, he says. His entire demeanour has changed. Like a light switched off. Looking anywhere but her.

She feels cold. Brings a hand to his cheek. He still does not look at her. She pushes her mouth onto his.

Ugh. A male voice in her head. A caricature of a French accent. *So desperate*, Gustave is saying. *Ugh.*

—

Jenny, her boyfriend and the unattractive one are talking to someone new. The girl from sixth form. Now she knows exactly who it is. She wants to leave, but she has been seen. The unattractive one is by her side, gesturing, pulling her by the arm. Here she is. This is my French mate. But she won't speak French for me.

She jerks her arm away.

Jenny's forehead wrinkles.

Oh, I know you, the girl says. You went to SEEC as well, didn't you?

The unattractive one is staring at her.

Did you go to that art school you were always going on about?

She looks over her shoulder, wanting to escape.

What was it called again?

The Slade, Jenny offers, eyes fixed on her. She works in London now.

Oh yeah? The girl's Essex accent is strong. Me too. Whereabouts?

Just. Just in London Bridge, she says.

Where, though.

She considers what to reveal. Just some B2B place, she says eventually.

The girl nods as though interested, but her eyes are narrowed. I remember from day dot you were going on and on about going to some fancy school for *artistes*.

She is being mocked.

I remember you making some crap art.

Jenny's mouth stretches, stuck between sympathy and mirth. Everyone else laughs.

To leave now would be to admit defeat. She inhales, straightens her neck. Well, you dropped out, she says.

The girl's face does not change. My mum got ill.

Oh, Jenny says.

She's dead now. The girl looks at her again. Couldn't all follow our dreams, could we? Not that I wanted to go to art school or anything. Did my apprenticeship in business management though, and I'm working in recruitment now, aren't I.

There is something about the girl's posture – chin lifted, shoulders back – which suggests that *working in recruitment* means she earns a lot of money.

The attractive one is nowhere. Maybe he left.

The unattractive one is squinting and appears to be genuinely puzzled. Wait. So you went to college here? When did you come to England?

Jenny holds up a hand. Wait, what are you talking about?

She's French. She told me.

Jenny's boyfriend asks what is happening.

The girl from college is laughing. Really laughing. Slapping a hand on her thigh. Honestly, I'm just cracking up. Always thought you were weird. You were always stuck-up.

It happens so quickly. She grabs the unattractive one's full pint from the table. She feels the weight of the glass in her hand. She watches the thrust of her arm, the liquid for a moment suspended in mid-air, then coating the girl's face, running down her chin, sluicing down her neck. The girl's face is screwed up. False eyelashes drenched.

What the fuck.

Oh my god, Jenny is saying, What the—

But now her eyes are filled with stinging wine. Warm liquid down her neck. The girl's arm is still outstretched.

Whoa, whoa. Jenny's boyfriend intervenes, his hand on her

shoulder. She shrugs it off, her hands investigating her wet cheeks, her eyes. Is her make-up running? Opposite her, the girl is receiving a lot of attention, and saying, Nah, I'm alright, I'm good, I'm good, get me another one, yeah?

Jenny wants her to come to the bathroom. Seemingly despite herself. No, she replies. Sticky and cold now the adrenaline has worn off. The butt of her hands against her face, she presses forward through everyone. As she passes the girl, she tries to shoulder her out of the way.

Are you fucking mad, the girl shouts, shoving her with a flat palm. Everyone is watching. She keeps walking, pushing through, pretending it did not hurt. She makes it to the pub doors. Hand, arm, half of her body landing against the door to push it open. She falls out into the night.

In her mind, Gustave looms: observing her from his commercial headshot. She is covered in Pinot Grigio and running. He is laughing at her. Of course he is. She is *tragic*.

Standing in her kitchenette she chews on a thumbnail, watching YouTube videos of Françoise Hardy. She refuses to think about what happened. Like it had happened to someone else and not her. A burning sensation rises up from the inside of her gum at the left of her mouth, sinking through into her skull. She brings a hand against it automatically, as if to push out the pain. She pushes the heel of her hand harder against her jaw, wanting to push the poison out through her nervous system and out of her body.

She starts going through her wardrobe and drawers, pulling out items, making outfits in neutral colours, in monochrome. *Keeping your wardrobe to neutral staples means it is easy to get dressed and look put-together.*

FUN ACCESSORIES ALLOW YOU TO PLAY DRESS-UP!

SIMPLICITY, MODESTY AND FEMININITY ARE KEY!

KEEP AN INTEREST IN FASHION BUT DON'T BECOME A VICTIM TO IT.

ABOVE ALL, SIMPLY RELAX AND ENJOY LIFE!

Navy and white. Black and white. Black and navy. She arranges each outfit onto a coat hanger, then hooks them over the door frame, bedposts, cupboards. Running out of hangers and space, she lays outfits on the floor, multiple two-dimensional versions of her on the carpet. She is surrounded by invisible bodies now. Everything else she bundles into bin bags. It takes several trips to dump all the bags on the street outside. She leaves her flat with her work bag, overstuffed.

TIME'S UP! For _Hay Fever_. TIME'S UP! For _Hay Fever_. TIME'S UP! For _Hay Fever_. TIME'S UP! For _Hay Fever_. TIME'S UP! For _Hay Fever_. TIME'S UP! For _Hay Fever_. TIME'S UP! For _Hay Fever_. TIME'S UP! For _Hay Fever_. TIME'S UP! For _Hay Fever_. TIME'S UP! For _Hay Fever_. TIME'S UP! For _Hay Fever_. TIME'S UP! For _Hay Fever_. TIME'S UP! For _Hay Fever_. TIME'S UP! For _Hay Fever_. TIME'S UP! For _Hay Fever_. TIME'S UP! For _Hay Fever_. TIME'S UP! For _Hay Fever_.

The train jerks forward and she steadies her bag on the seat beside her. She passes through towns, the names and sequence she knows by heart – black against a violet dawn. The Eurostar website says the next train with seats available from St Pancras International to Paris Gare du Nord is in three hours. Two hundred and sixty-seven pounds. One-way. She books it on her credit card and receives the ticket confirmation. She opens a new tab and googles Gustave, skipping forwards to page thirty-two of the image results.

At St Pancras International, people queue, dead-eyed. She picks out which ones are French from the shape of their mouths, pulled back to contort vowels and swallow the consonants. She clears her throat, envisioning how her face will move when she speaks in French, as if it will come naturally to her the moment she is in Paris. Her core, something in her core, vibrates with new energy. Yes, she thinks. Yes. This is right.

The automated announcements shatter against the glass walls, the glass roof. The artificial light is very white. She looks at her phone and googles the Op-Us website.

Operation: Us. Together. Our story. Our mission. Our team. Our offices. Addresses in Paris, Munich, Brussels. Gustave, Director of Sales for all these places, so much geographical spread to his name. She sees Gustave walking into each office, occasionally mentioning the woman he met in London. Will people know how young and beautiful she is? Will he show them photos of her? Then she sees herself on his arm at work events, wearing something simple but elegant, hair and make-up just right. His colleagues whisper among themselves, admiring but equally scorned because he has chosen her over them. Then she drops by the office with a lovely baby in a pram, saying, I'm just dropping by to see Gustave. In French, obviously. He greets her in front of everyone, affectionate to the appropriate level, just enough so everyone sees how pleased he is to see her, how his face softens, how he softens for her and no one else. Walking down the platform to her carriage, at her core there is now a glowing particle, a radiant atom.

Her seat choice was forward-facing. The decision seemed fundamental, no longer watching the past as it disappears but moving forwards, seeing only new things. She holds her phone tightly in her lap. She is leaving. It feels definitive. Mentally farewelling things on the other side of the window. The platform. The other trains. The vast station. The buildings beyond. The grey sun. London. Datata. Making coffee for arseholes. Fenchurch Street. The commute. Paying four hundred pounds a month for the pleasure. Southend. Jenny. The cafe that only takes cash and does avocado on toast and Buck's Fizz like it's 2012. Those pubs. The people. That girl in the pub with her screwed-up face. Goodbye to all that. There is an announcement in English and then in French. Now the train has started, its motion near silent. She looks out of the window. She is moving towards everything. Everything is moving towards her.

London flips between glass and metal and brick, a glitching simulation of this world. Then countryside. Kent. She laughs to herself. Miles of Kent. Then the windows switch to black and this world has come to an end.

She turns to her newly sharpened reflection. The eyes meet her own in the darkness. A version of herself with healthy-looking skin and relaxed shoulders, wearing a blue dress, stands waiting for her on the beach.

PARIS

She wakes. The train is slowing. People unfurl from their seats. Her phone has adjusted to French time: an hour swallowed. Time travel.

She steps off the train and out into French air. It is warmer and more fragrant, she thinks. It just smells French. Outside the station entrance, the streets are wide, the buildings old, grand but not tall, the sky wide and open, leaving space for her to breathe. The trees are full-leafed and stirring gently. It is better here, better than anywhere. She sees herself from the outside: someone arriving in Paris to see her French lover. Sunlight obscures the passing faces. She feels in control of her body, which is now thin and long-limbed. Let them look, she thinks.

She arrives at the lobby of the three-star hotel she booked on her phone. There is a cigarette machine and a teenage boy wearing a T-shirt behind the reception desk.

Bonjour. J'ai un booking. Because The French always say bonjour first.

The boy looks at her once, then at the booking confirmation email on the screen of her phone, which she has held up to him automatically.

Passport, he says.

She obliges, accepting the boy's offhand attitude because she is also nonchalant and French. He looks at it and nods. Places a key on the desk.

The hotel room is sparse: white walls, a carpet which looks as though it was once patterned. A patch of something which might be mould trailing down from one corner. Bohemian, she thinks, flicking through the instant coffee sachets, imagining Gustave admiring how content she is with its simplicity. The energy of Gustave's gaze has changed; now alkaline, not acid. They are one. If she flattens her body against the windowsill, the road below is visible. She opens the window, hears sirens, cars beeping. Perched on the window ledge, she stares down at a man's scalp as he strides down the pavement. French people even look good from a distance. She has an urge to bolt from the room, run down the stairs and follow him. Here, she could have anyone.

Late afternoon settles in slowly, the sinking sun reflected in the office building that contains the Op-Us office and several other digital businesses. She walks up the steps to the building entrance. It is Sunday. All the lights are off. Across the wide road – the boulevard – there is a cafe, chairs and tables stacked inside, crimson awning drawn in. She will sit outside here tomorrow and wait for Gustave, catch him off guard on his way into the office. How surprised he will be to see her! Surprise, she will say. Or Surprise! pronounced the French way.

She returns to the hotel with a bag of unknown leaves – because for French women, beauty starts on the inside – bought from a mini supermarket, with a feeling she considers labelling euphoria for the way the cashier had mumbled to her and how she had responded in kind, eyes downcast, just another Parisian doing their shopping. And now France 24 is on the television as she is sitting cross-legged on the bed, shovelling leaves into her mouth, willing herself to acquire the language.

Her phone vibrates from somewhere. She looks at the screen. Javier. She chews a handful of leaves into a lump in her mouth, juices moving against her teeth. A news ident announces the arrival of a blonde presenter, who is wearing pearl earrings. Chic.

Javier calls again.

Bonjour, she answers, still chewing.

Hey. Javier's voice crackles. How are you? He already sounds pathetic.

I'm in Paris, she says.

You're what?

In Paris.

A red ident sweeps across the screen. The blonde presenter turns to someone at the other end of the table. An intense discussion begins.

What are you doing there?

To see my boyfriend. He's from here.

A second of silence in which she estimates Javier's disappointment. When did you get a boyfriend, he says.

She eats more leaves. Don't know what to tell you, Javier. I met him and it was pretty much love at first sight. For both of us, she says. We just connect, like, so well.

Oh yeah? Better than we did?

There wasn't a connection with us, Javier. Just your ideas about who I am. What you wanted from me.

Another short silence from Javier. I was just calling to see how you are. Things ended badly. But. I guess that doesn't matter now.

She pulls a face, for her own benefit as Javier cannot see it. There were no things. We were never a thing.

On the television a man with short hair and a long nose adjusts his metal-framed glasses, looking serious.

Can I have my phone back?

Nope. She examines a leaf stem in her fingers, carved out from between her teeth. Flicks the stem away. Anyway, got to go. Bisous.

After disconnecting the call, she pushes the phone across the bed, watching the B-movie horror poster slide across the duvet and onto the floor. She turns up the television. The blonde presenter disappears behind another ident. The images of news events are interrupted by a burst of pain as her rotting tooth rubs against the one below like grinding stone. She presses her hand against her cheek, eyes still on France 24. Focuses. Counts the recognizable words rolling across the screen. Affaires. Actions. Circulation. Diffusion. Transaction. Opération.

Lying in bed, she holds the phone above herself. Blue light cast down onto her face in the dark. A YouTube video of French people being approached in the streets of Paris and asked what they, as French people, think of French stereotypes. A teenage girl flicks her hair, shrugging, looking away, heavily accented: I, uh… don't know, you know? A man with folded arms and sunglasses laughs, stepping back: Oh, I'm not actually French. The interviewer, hidden behind the camera, plays it up. You're not? No, no. I'm German. Well, you look very French, I must say. Thank you.

She pictures herself, the American thrusting a microphone beneath her chin and asking what she thinks of French stereotypes. She wears sunglasses and does not remove them. She flicks her hair, shrugging, looking away: I, uh… don't know, you know?

She opens Gustave's Twitter feed. His last tweet was on Friday. *So excited to be partnering with Datata to distribute our new Platinum Protection Plus. It really is the dream product for all of your business encryption needs. #encryption #operation-us.* She cannot see who has liked it because she does not have a Twitter account. She presses the heart anyway, numbly receiving the prompt to sign up, getting as far as being sent a confirmation email to activate her new account when the entire process suddenly seems arduous, too big, and too desperate.

Early next morning she spends thirty-seven minutes deciding what to wear. She brought just one pair of elegant flats, which work for every occasion. There is a surge in her chest, so strong and good-tasting that she has the urge to give her mirror reflection the finger-guns. She considers whether this would be an Amélie thing to do. Decides it would not be. She leaves her key on the reception desk, calling out merci to no response.

At the cafe facing the Op-Us building, she takes off her bag and sits at an outside table, at first with her arms laid on either side of the chair and then bringing her arms down, not knowing what to do with them, letting them fall awkwardly into her lap. Sensing she is being watched, she turns to see the waiter standing close by, his face white and creased in the sun. Black coffee, she says. Please.

The waiter nods, raps on a table twice with his knuckles and goes back into the cafe. She regrets not having asked in French. Un café noir, s'il vous plaît. So easy.

People in office wear approach the building opposite. Her stomach contracts with the thought of seeing him.

A black coffee arrives in front of her. Then a London number appears on her phone. Datata. She stares at it until the call ends. A voicemail symbol appears. She puts the phone in her bag and lights a cigarette. She brings the coffee to her lips and its heat spreads into her gums, pain immediately rising from her back tooth. She squashes her free palm against her cheek, reciting a mantra to herself until the pain subsides: I am drinking coffee outside a cafe in Paris. I am drinking coffee outside a cafe in Paris. I will see Gustave soon. I am drinking coffee in Paris. I will see Gustave soon. In Paris. Gustave soon, in Paris, where I am now. Drinking coffee outside.

The sun is a little higher in the sky. More people. More cars. Scooters and motorbikes speeding, jumping kerbs. No Gustave yet. Coffee cup long empty, gritty dregs in the bottom. Then the flow of bodies thins out. People walk with less urgency. The workday has started. The waiter is at her side again.

Le bill? she asks.

He pulls a small piece of paper from his notebook and places it on the table before her.

She shows her card.

He says something. Her mind attempts to translate it. He says it again. She stares at him.

Only cash, he says in English.

She knows her purse is empty but she will make a show of looking inside it anyway. She picks up her bag and unzips it on her lap. A part of her wishes he would take pity on her. This seems unlikely. Her face grows hot. Grasping for anything, she finds a spare pair of underwear, chewing gum, a broken cigarette. Her rummaging is interrupted by a voice. The waiter turns at the waist, gesturing for the voice to wait. The voice says something else. The waiter lifts a finger before her face, communicating for her to wait, then walks away to attend to the other customer.

She shoves back her chair in one decisive motion and it scroops against the concrete. She walks, then runs, out into the wide road, a motorbike screeching around her, the driver shouting something she doesn't need to understand. She keeps running, raising her palm to a car, which does not stop for her. Then to another car coming in the other direction. A scooter stops for her, allowing her to finally reach the other side of the street. Then up the steps towards the office building. The automated doors part, and she is inside. It is air-conditioned and silent. A security guard stares at her. She hopes to come across as cheerful and not manic. A sign by a lift says Op-Us are on the fourth floor. As she approaches, the lift opens as if waiting for her. She strides in. The doors close. Clearing her throat, she brushes herself down, bringing a hand to her jaw, bringing it away again, ruffling her hair, smoothing it down, straightening her back. The doors open. The fourth floor is so brightly lit it appears to have almost no depth. She goes to the white reception desk on the left. To one side there is a bowl of ornamental glass stones. It strikes her, violently, how tacky and kitsch the stones look, how out of place. As the receptionist looks up from her laptop and returns her gaze, she experiences a flash of vertigo, feeling that her cover has been blown: that somehow the receptionist recognizes her as a receptionist too.

Is Gustave here?

Hrmm? Pardon?

Her fingers tighten around her bag strap. Gustave. She pronounces it in a more exaggerated way. Gustave Caron?

Do you have an appointment?

I'm his partner.

Sorry. The receptionist pulls a self-deprecating expression. My English is—

I'm his partner. Girlfriend. I know him. It comes from her forcefully.

The receptionist's face opens up with understanding. Of course. I am so sorry. We have not met before.

She puts on a relaxed smile, thinking about how her eyes shine under the fluorescent lights. Gustave's lovely partner.

Sorry, your name. It is Christine, yes?

She feels her mouth open, close, then open again. What?

Christine. The receptionist is showing teeth, expectant. You are Christine. Gustave's, uh, wife. Non?

Her stomach plummets. She feels clammy. Dizzy. This is a mistake. This must be a mistake. A mistake is happening somewhere. The receptionist's face fades out, disappears. It is too loud in here. Telephones and people talking. Those glass stones are so tacky, garish.

Yes, she says, mouth dry. Yes. I am Christine.

Her face is burning hot.

Okay. But he is in a meeting. Please — the receptionist is standing now, coming around the desk and extending an arm to direct her — come with me.

She presses her lips together. She is being led somewhere beyond reception, entering space with people working at desks, past glass offices. The ceiling is low and the fluorescent lights are too bright. The receptionist waves to someone, says something in French. That inner plummet again. The dizziness. Where is she going? Is she going to be presented to Gustave in front of everyone? Is it too late. Could she turn and run. People look up, inquisitive eyes. She looks away. It is too late. Everyone has seen her now.

The receptionist approaches a door at the end of the passage, holding it open for her. You can wait here?

It is a small meeting room, with two chairs and a low table. There are no windows. It is like the waiting room of a funeral home.

The receptionist says something. She turns.

A drink?

She shakes her head. Mouth dry but not wanting. Not daring.

The receptionist lets go of the door and it closes her in.

Her heartbeat makes itself known over the muffled chattering sounds through the walls. She sits down, assuming this is the right thing to do in this situation. Steadies her hands before her. Inhales. Exhales. Then gets out her phone.

Christine Caron is easy to find online. On her LinkedIn she wears a navy suit jacket, gives the camera a relaxed smile. Arms crossed to show long fingers holding herself, with a simple and elegant manicure. She is white, with short brown hair. Really nice hair. Brown eyes. Her skin has a peach glow. And a public Instagram account: her life is too good not to share. There are photos in which she looks away from the camera, to the side or down demurely; all angles which accentuate the beautiful shape of her nose, a smooth curve with a quiet ending, laughing at the person to whom her eyes are directed. In all of them: white teeth and sunsets, hair still really nice despite an obvious breeze. She is a traveller: filtered photos of Vietnam, Cuba, Tunisia. A foodie: photos of small and expensive meals. Two glasses of wine on the table. Scrolling down, there is a photo of Christine with someone else. She is wearing a wedding dress. Simple, elegant. Something which might be called A-line, or empire or whatever, the necessity of this information feeling like an extra locking-out as her eyes translate the male figure in the photo as Gustave, who is wearing a suit, the groom to the bride. Uploaded in 2019.

She pictures Christine undressing at the end of the day, undressing before Gustave, in their beautiful home together. Gustave, who looks at her and loves her. Gustave taking those long and immaculate fingers in his own and marrying her. She must wake up glowing every day. It's genetics, people say, it's your bone structure. But really, Christine is made beautiful with the love of Gustave.

She does not notice the door opening, does not notice until he is standing there at the edge of the room. His black eyes wide. Laptop bag in one hand. Arms at slight angles outwards, poised. What might have been a smile on his face is now on its way to something else, frozen mid-transition. The room seems to shrink. She tries to breathe. The door closes slowly with a managed, hushed click. Gustave continues trying to find his face. Strains for a commercial smile, relaxed and unoffended. But this falters as his eyes roll downwards, drawn to something. He is looking at her phone, screen up in her hand. The photo of his wedding day. What is, uh. What is that, he says.

She turns the phone over, concealing it, and says, Nothing.

He remains staring at the spot. His face has changed again, mouth a straight line. Then he looks to her. This is why you have come here? All the way here? An underline of anger.

She cannot look at him so she turns over the phone to see the image of smiling Gustave again. No. I just came here to see you.

What.

Now she looks at him. I just wanted to see you.

Gustave does something like a hard blink. Then he straightens, exhaling through his nostrils. This is quite intense, he says.

Are you still married?

He brings a hand to his eyes, rubbing them. We cannot talk about this here.

His eyes flick away. She is an annoyance. Yes we can, she says.

No. This is my place of work and it is not appropriate.

Why not. You came on to me at my place of work.

His eyes narrow. Are you serious?

Are you going to leave her?

Gustave gives a short laugh, shaking his head, looking at his shoes. Saying, Oh my god.

You wouldn't cheat on her if you didn't want me instead, would you? You wouldn't have.

She is talking fast. Guts unravelling.

Gustave brings one hand out of his pocket, then does nothing with it.

What do you even like about her? She looks boring as fuck.

She holds up the wedding photo, hot in her hand, catching how Gustave looks briefly at it again despite himself. He is gathering his thoughts. I'm sorry, he says, but I think you have misunderstood the situation.

No, she says. No, I haven't.

Please, he is saying now.

She stands, dashing the phone to the floor. There is a single cracking sound. Gustave makes a hushing motion, recoiling as she moves towards him, his shoulders rising in defence. You kissed me, she is saying. You kissed me. She tries to take hold of him, but he steps back before she can make contact. Her hands clasp around nothing. She steps forwards again, trying to get through to him. You can have me, she says, just—

The words end, knocked out of her chest by Gustave's forearm. She falls back and lands against the low table, ungainly, pathetic. The impact travels up her spine. She wants to cry out but resists, clamping her mouth shut. From the floor she sees a new Gustave, his eyes wild, glaring, arm stuck out before him, arrested mid-movement. She grasps behind for something to pull herself up with, finding a hold on the chair.

Sorry, he says.

Her skull feels heavy. Tears gather. She withholds them. The qualities a Frenchman looks for in a woman: integrity, intelligence, personality, quick wit, generosity, forgiving. She sits back down on the floor, letting go of the chair. No. No, I'm sorry. I shouldn't be here. Can we. Can we talk later?

It's not— Gustave stops, recalibrates. I don't think this is a good idea.

Then what. Then what do we do?

He does not say anything.

I'm not leaving, she says. Covers her face to hide her tears.

When she takes them away, Gustave is gone. She stays where she is, the air conditioning running cold. What now. What now. What now.

The door opens and the receptionist appears. Oh, Christine. Everything is okay?

She sniffs, scratching the back of her neck, trying to look casual.

Gustave asked me to book you a taxi. He says you're going back to England. Charles de Gaulle, it is okay for you?

She notices how young the receptionist looks, how stupid she looks. Wet behind the ears. She must do anything Gustave asks. Get his lunch order. Get his coffee. Get a taxi to deliver this hag elsewhere.

She stands, using the chair for leverage. Gathers up her phone, looks at the damage, adjusts her bag strap, smooths herself down.

He does this all the time.

Pardon?

She is already moving, wedging herself between the receptionist and the open door. The receptionist shrinks back. She walks out, tipping her chin upwards to deflect the gazes of everyone around, who she is sure are looking at her in a different way now. At the reception desk she stops, steps back a few paces. The ugly glass stones in their stupid glass bowl. She shoves her fingers into them and throws a handful against the wall, where the Op-Us sign is mounted in metal lettering. It is like the sound of a sudden rainstorm.

—

Paris smudges around her, now an alien place with an alien atmosphere. A body shoves into her. Something is said in her direction. She walks without awareness until the air changes, a body of water appearing before her. A tour boat bubbles along the surface. Gustave. Gustave would never take a tour boat. Well, neither would she. The thought of jumping into the river. Jumping into the Seine. How French it would be. Nobody bearing witness except for the idiot tourists on the idiot boat. Images of her body being lifted from the water on France 24. A beautiful corpse. Or left leaking dark on the concrete from beneath a white sheet. Featureless, a blob, or worse: bloated. But Gustave unseeing and uncaring now anyway. The thought of returning to Southend is worse than killing herself. She steps up and onto the wall.

Bodies are speaking in tones of some urgency at her elbow.

It's fine. She steps down from the wall. It's fine. I wasn't going to jump. I said, I wasn't going to jump. Get off me.

She goes through two bottles of red wine that taste gratifyingly like mud, drinking them in the corner of a square, pigeons encroaching at her feet, a woman in several coats watching on. At the end of the first bottle, she has a clear thought: if she cannot go back, then she must stay. She books another hotel, prepays until the weekend, not looking long enough to see the price, only knowing that this one is four stars, because fuck you Gustave. The interior looks elegant, with ornamental fittings and real plants. She can take photographs of herself here and post them online. My new life in Paris. A text arrives from her phone contract provider about roaming charges. A tourist, two tourists, a couple, flinch at her nearness and she swears at them. She drinks the second bottle walking along narrow streets, peering into shops, staring down her reflection in the windows. She buys a third bottle from the Carrefour she was in yesterday, not saying hello or please or thank you or goodbye in French or English. She tucks it under her arm, lights a cigarette and thinks that, if she has nothing else, at least she looks cool and troubled.

At the new hotel she holds onto the reception desk to keep herself steady. When she cracks jokes, feeling like an animated gargoyle, the immaculate receptionist smiles tightly. The room is on the eighth floor. She has been in enough lifts and the thought of the sudden upward motion makes her feel unwell. She decides to take the stairs to her new room. As she reaches a door with a gilded number eight, she stops and her heart rises to her throat. She is breathing loudly, sweating. Her legs ache. Why is this hotel so hot? The corridors are dark. Bland photos of the Paris skyline hang on the walls. It takes five minutes to find the room. Upon finding it and slapping the key card onto the sensor, she finds that the room is exactly like the hotel room in which she met Gustave. As if they are part of the same chain. You're having a laugh, she says to herself, throwing her bag and the now empty wine bottle down somewhere. She collapses, half landing on the bed and needing to pull herself up with the top sheet bunched in both hands. She pushes her whole face into the mattress, feeling the cartilage of her nose resist. And screams.

The contents of the toilet bowl are too abject to be any closer to. Dizziness swirls from her eyes to her stomach. I'm not going to be sick again. I'm not going to be sick again. I'm not going to be sick again. She spits.

A knock.

She spits again.

Knock-knock.

Just a… The words come out gagged. In the hallway, a hoover starts up. The roar is too much. She groans with it. Tries to steady herself, to stand up straight. She remembers, having idly read somewhere online, that seasickness is worse when you're down in the cabin, down in the bottom.

She wakes up to her phone rattling on the bedside table. A London number. The time is 11:12.

Hello? The words come out sticky and slow, her lips making a pat-pat noise.

Just woken up have we.

The room is too bright. She fell asleep without closing the curtains.

Who's this?

Wow, you really have just woken up.

Rolling it over in her mind. Oscar. Oscar slapping the backs of other men. Oh, she says. Oh.

Yes. Oh. Are you planning to come into work at all?

Blinking. And when blinking doesn't help, she closes her eyes. I can't. I, erm. I told Jerry that I'm not well.

You told Jerry. Oscar is saying this pointedly. If you're going to be absent, you let your line manager know before you're due to start.

But I told Jerry, she lies again.

He's the em-dee, not your line manager. I'm your line manager.

In her mind there is an image of Oscar standing at his desk, weighted glances to others, pulling faces for his entertainment and theirs. Everybody in on the joke. Oscar has his flaccid cock on the desk, hands on hips.

I find it concerning that you've been here, for what, six months now? And—

Seven.

What's that?

It's seven months.

Sure. And your conduct is already becoming pretty subpar. Turning up late. And now unauthorized absences. I should be going straight to your agency with this, shouldn't I.

A pigeon flies past the window, gliding with a dead expression.

I can't make it in this week.

And why's that?

I'm unwell.

Can I ask why you're unwell?

What. What does that mean. I'm just ill. Is that okay with you. Do not speak to me like that.

Professional Oscar. A second in which her stomach tightens. She sits up and says, I'm going to complain to HR.

The room is hot and dry. Oscar's words are spaced out as though she does not understand English. Sorry, what did you say?

I'm going to HR because I have been experiencing sexual harassment from a senior member of one of Datata's partners.

Four seconds.

Sorry?

Gustave Caron from Op-Us. He came on to me. In the office.

Is that true?

Why do you think I'm off sick?

She hears him breathe. A pigeon flies past in the opposite direction, possibly the same pigeon as before.

And he's married, she presses. So he's cheated on his wife as well. But that's by the by, obviously.

Oscar starts speaking with a loose, high tone, Who, Chri— Then he stops. Starting again with his professional voice. Sexual harassment is a very serious allegation that needs to be investigated via the correct channels.

Are you not the correct channels?

She imagines the people around Oscar, previously grinning along with him, now falling silent, glancing at him with concern, everyone embarrassed. He puts away his cock.

If you don't believe me, she says, I'll just tell Jerry.

No. No. It is my duty now to handle this disclosure—

I don't want it to be investigated.

You don't want it to be investigated, he repeats back.

No. I just needed to tell you. Now you know. It will be on the security cameras though, from Thursday. In the kitchen. If you still don't believe me.

Okay. So, look. Oscar hopefully putting a hand to his face, pinching the top of his nose, looking tired. Send me an email. Just say you're taking the week off due to. To personal reasons as discussed. No need to go into details. We'll talk when you come back.

I mean. It's a shame that Gustave felt comfortable enough to start harassing female members of Data staff so early into the new partnership. I hope this doesn't cause any issues between you and ruin your… what would you call it? Friendship?

Oscar hangs up.

In the window she sees the collar of her shirt, unchanged from yesterday. Her reflection, faint with no head.

She stands outside the hotel. It is raining. A fine rain. Gustave is showing up as online on WhatsApp. He must be thinking of her in some way. Surely he would block her if this was not the case. If whatever was between them was done.

She walks towards what Google Maps has told her is the centre of Paris. Through a commercial area with designer stores, street vendors, steam rising from their hotplates. She keeps walking, recrossing the river each time she finds a bridge. Things pass, things which seem familiar, as though she has been here before, or seen them before. Statues of people on horses, lions. A pointy monument. Things she ought to know the name of. Why? It is just Paris. It is just Paris, she thinks.

A park appears on her left. She enters. The space opens up with wide shingled paths, leading to a luminous green lake. Tourists in raincoats look nervously at the sky. People jog in Lycra. She walks around the edge of the lake, keeps walking until she comes across a large sculpture in the middle of a square of grass, the form of a naked woman turned on her side, attached to the plinth by her hip, her skin the greenish grey of lead – a woman wrestled down by some invisible force, her hands held up to it, legs bent. A woman in free fall. Head tilted, hanging over the edge of the plinth, mouth open, lips turned downwards in a grimace. Eyes blank as the eyes of sculptures are.

She takes a photo of the sculpture. There is the sound of thunder and the tourists look more worried. Wanders the city until she finds an art shop. She picks up a sketchbook and pencils. They are expensive. She is certain her debit card will be turned down. There is a beat before she reads Approuvée on the machine. A tightness makes itself known on its release in her chest.

Back at the hotel, there is a man behind the reception desk this time. She feels a familiar irk as he looks her up and down. He nods to the sketchbook held under her arm. You are an artist?

No, she says, not stopping to see his reaction.

Over her shoulder, behind her, he starts to laugh. Ha ha ha ha ha.

She sleeps all afternoon. When she wakes, she climbs across the bed and takes up the sketchbook and pencils from the desk. She draws the sculpture from the photo on her phone. It has been a long time since she last held a pencil. But the strength in the joints is easy to capture. Easy to make her own. The pencil leaves tender welts on her fingers. Then she flicks to the next blank page and begins to draw Gustave's face from memory, making lines to suggest an ear, then the mole beside it. This time the result is clumsy, awkward. She tries starting with the lines of his forehead, on another page that commercial smile, on another page his wide nose, on another page the square of his jaw. But the features are continuously not-right, not-Gustave.

What is it that you want to achieve? A question asked of her continuously by her tutors at art school. What is it that you want to achieve? Is this something you aim to explore? And with this pressure to justify her work, over time the satisfaction of things coming together – textures moving the right way, forms with the right balance – became harder to reach. Her hands started to fail her. Her housemates, whose parents paid their fees and rent, talked about freelance opportunities while she tried to sleep, her alarm set for the next temping job.

She opens Christine's Instagram and scrolls to the wedding photo, thinking that all good artists use references. But she realizes after an unknown number of seconds that she is not looking at Gustave at all – she is looking at Christine. She screenshots the image so that she can zoom in without accidentally hitting the like icon. Christine's lips are full, parting in the middle, a natural pout, as though she were about to speak. Knowingly assured. Her décolletage even and unblemished. She tears out the sketchbook page. Folds it once. Bites off the corner. Scrunches every other not-Gustave in her hand. Fits a whole ball of paper into her mouth and bites down hard. Her mouth hangs open, drooling. A corner pokes into her rotten cavity, and the pain begins.

Outside the hotel the atmosphere is fragrant with dirt and bread. As she walks along the street, the buildings around her alternately shade her from and expose her to the sun. What else is there to do in Paris except walk? It is the art of exploring the city. There is a flower stall, with some type of flower she recognizes but does not know the name of, in two colours, deep red and yellow. A woman with a French girl bob looks at her.

Next to the stall is a pharmacy. At the counter she asks for ibuprofen and adds s'il vous plait. The pharmacist asks her a question, in perfect but accented English, and with a stern and maternal manner which is disarming. She identifies the mal, pushing a finger into her cheek, poking at the cavity. Realizing she is gurning, she retrieves the finger quickly and rubs it dry against her top. The pharmacist advises that if there is pain then she may have an infection, and that she must make an appointment with her dentist, otherwise she may need surgery.

The box of tablets is placed on the counter. Card machine presented. She brings out her card and presses it to the machine. There comes a disapproving beep: the payment has not worked. Busy elsewhere, the pharmacist appears not to have noticed.

She slowly puts her hand around the ibuprofen box.

A bell pings from the door as she leaves. She runs. Back down the street, past the flower stall, a golden version of herself flashing past in parallel. Round a corner, she stops and slaps two capsules from her palm to her mouth. She moves her tongue to create saliva. While trying to swallow, she looks at her phone. The photo of Gustave and Christine is still open. She scrolls down to the comments. Twenty-three. Congratulations in French, English. She stops at one.

So beautiful! Heart-eyes emoji *Ndn Crn.*

Ndn. She looks closely at the thumbnail image of the girl. Something about the flash of forehead. Strong, flat eyebrows. Dark eyes. She enlarges the image with her thumb and index finger. The girl is turned at an angle to disguise a potentially wide nose. Dark eyes set heavily. The girl looks thoughtful. Ndn Crn. She rattles through the girl's Instagram posts. Photos of classical paintings, the girl standing outside a museum or gallery. The girl and her friends, artfully blurred, pulling the peace sign.

Until finally one causes everything to stop. Taken from a lower angle, a bright sun and blue sky behind. The girl is close to the camera, showing freckles, face cuddled into the shoulder of an older man. The girl's hair is swept back, the dry stiff texture of the loose strands suggesting the presence of salt water. Both are wearing sunglasses. At first she doesn't recognize the man. Then she spots the mole by his ear, lifted by the grin in his cheek. Of course: she did not recognize him because he is smiling so widely. Unguarded. Dimples in his stubble, the grey flecks glowing in the sun. The caption: *moi et ma papa stupide.*

Emojis: a palm tree, an ocean wave. Fifty-seven likes and ten comments. *NADINE MA MEUF!!!!* heart-eyes emoji heart-eyes emoji heart-eyes emoji

Gustave and his daughter, Nadine.

She closes her eyes, the image of Nadine Caron imprinted in the darkness.

In the morning, she showers, noticing that the micellar water seems to be changing the texture of her face.

She sits in the hotel restaurant and takes two ibuprofen with coffee. Craving sugar, she empties one sachet into her coffee cup. She stirs it in while looking out of the window. Then she takes another sachet.

The receptionist who laughed at her yesterday has already annoyed her again this morning, encouraging her towards the breakfast buffet. It is an extra twenty euros. She declined, saying she was not hungry. Now he is approaching her again, holding out a white paper bag. You said you were not hungry, he says. But just in case. On the house.

She watches the gold rings on his fingers move as he releases the bag into her hand. He tries to catch her eye and succeeds briefly. The skin beneath his eyes is grey. His gold-coloured name tag says Ismail. She can feel that the contents of the paper bag are warm.

She is surprised to find Nadine still has a Facebook account. The profile is bare, defunct, yet public, revealing her age – 17 – and the school she attends: lycée-something-something-bi-lingualism-something. She finds it on Google Maps. It could almost be another apartment building, except that it has a thick black gate. Further down the cobbled pavement, there is a slim tree with a white trunk. She looks at other photos of the school. It has a large outdoor area, with a basketball court, lined with railings and trees.

She looks up the directions. Just interested, she thinks. I'm just interested.

—

Sitting on a bench outside the school, she says to herself, If I just see her, that will be enough.

She watches teenagers walk up the street towards the thick black gate, wearing jeans, their hair moving freely, Roman noses. Nadine must speak English as naturally as a stream. What if she was to know Nadine and Nadine know her? The possibility vibrates through her.

Three young people approach, two boys and a girl. The boy with a shaved head has his arm around the the girl's shoulder. They pass beneath a tree. When they emerge from the shade, the girl's hair catches sunlight like fire and her face becomes clear.

She must be staring, because the young girl is looking at her. Big dark eyes. Expression opening like a door.

Excusez. Duolingo has told her this is the proper French way to say excuse-moi.

The boy with his arm around Nadine is forced to stop. The other boy, walking ahead, glances back and frowns.

The hugeness of the situation lands. She fiddles absent-mindedly with her hands. Sorry, I. Erm. Do you speak English?

Nadine blinks. Yes.

Okay. She pulls out a smile. Okay, that's cool. I've just been watching you. She gestures to the bench behind her, pretending there is nothing special about this, no hot dread creeping up her neck.

Watching me? A sweetening American twang.

Yeah. You just. You seem interesting.

The words are bad. There is silence. A breeze. Nadine looks to her friends, mouth open, confused. The boy withdraws his arm and looks to the other boy with pursed lips. The other boy snorts, hands in his pockets, saying something which sounds like jaarrrrrrrr. Now both boys are laughing. Nadine gives a quick laugh, then brings a palm to her mouth as though it had escaped accidentally. The hugeness becomes a hole.

Sorry. She brings out a hand in the air between them. I know that sounds weird.

The boy furthest away bucks in the middle, shaking his head, then walks away into the school. Nadine tightens her mouth, then relaxes her face.

The remaining boy says, What do you want, crazy lady?

She gazes at Nadine again, who looks uncomfortable but is trying to hide it. Politeness or saving face. Arms folded, legs crossed at the ankle, her body slanted.

Well, I'm. I'm actually not a crazy lady. I'm an artist.

The boy is stumped for a second but then makes a so what? face, shrugging. Nadine looks to him then back to her, eyes the only thing moving.

An artist?

Yeah. I'm an artist. And I saw you, and I'm interested in you. There's. Well, I can like, draw people and things. A golden idea rushes towards her. She steadies herself, trying not to widen her eyes. Would you like to model for me?

Nadine looks uncertain. Um, she says, unfolding her arms and folding them again.

The boy is now talking to another girl walking towards them. The girl has long dark hair. They talk in French over the head of Nadine, who looks embarrassed and awkward.

Now the new girl is looking at her with suspicion. It feels like her blood is thickening.

Do you always wait outside schools looking at kids? the girl asks.

No. She does an amicable and relaxed laugh to suggest how ridiculous this reaction is. I was just. I look for subjects. So I was sitting here and soaking things in. That's what artists do. And I happened to see her. She turns to Nadine again. Sorry, I don't even know your name?

Nadine.

Her friends look at her quickly as though surprised. Nadine does not look at anyone.

Nadine, she repeats back, pronouncing it exactly right. Look, if you don't want to model for me, then it's no problem. I understand.

Everyone is staring at Nadine now, who shrugs, pulling at her jumper sleeve. The other girl, appearing to soften, brings a hand to Nadine's arm.

The boy turns to her and says, Prove it. Prove that you're an artist.

My sweet child, she thinks, if only you knew that I had to prove I was an artist every day for three years. She takes out her sketchbook from her bag. Opens it at the page with the drawing of the sculpture in the park. All three teenagers frown at it.

Then Nadine murmurs, Oh. I know it. It is La Rivière, no?

The one in the park, she responds, nodding. Their eyes meet directly. They are both nodding now, slowly, in a rhythm of understanding.

The boy, noticing the shared look between Nadine and the artist, asks if she can show them anything else.

Google me. She pulls out a pencil and writes on the corner of the page. Here's my name. And here's my phone number. She passes the slip of paper to Nadine, whose fingers emerge out of her baggy jumper sleeve. Think about it, she says. You would make a good model.

Nadine is still nodding slowly, straightening the paper between her thumbs.

It is just weird that you are out here, like, watching people, says the other girl.

She holds up her palms. Okay, I get it. It is weird. But you would be surprised how many of my models I find on the street.

They blink at her.

A lot, she makes clear.

We have a lot of warnings in school about, you know… The male friend's face thaws into something apologetic. Trafficking.

It's good that you look out for Nadine. If it helps, I'm only twenty-seven, so.

Traffickers can be any age, says the female friend, eyes scanning down her. And they are usually women and also well dressed. Like you.

Oh. Thanks.

The three teenagers turn and head towards the school gates, backpacks swinging on one shoulder.

She closes the sketchbook and puts it away. How easy that was. Returning to the bench, she thinks about the classical paintings Nadine posted online, appearing between countless photos of Nadine posing. She opens the white paper bag and pulls out a ham and cheese croissant. She picks out the ham and bites it. It is not ham. She slaps it onto the pavement. Pigeons land and tear at it, leaving behind a clammy stain. The bag also contains an apple, which she thinks about for ten minutes before chewing it slowly with one side of her mouth and then dropping it on the ground. The pigeons make a go of the core, tossing it about. How easy that was.

In the afternoon she sits at a pavement cafe and receives a message from a number with a French dialling code.

i couldn't find any of your work online…

She breathes in and out. Sips her coffee.

Hi Nadine! Great to hear from you. That's a shame you couldn't find anything. There should be something online about my degree show?

Nadine reads the message then no longer shows as online.

She orders another coffee, with milk this time. She drinks slowly, watching the foam pool in the bottom of the cup. She is nauseous with the caffeine.

Nadine writes again. *there was like one image of something you made like ten years ago.*

Ten years, lol! It was five years ago but I'll forgive you for that. But you're right, there's not a lot of my work online. Not since I went to art school. I went to the Slade, have you heard of it?

Nadine is typing.

yes. And then my friend is going to goldsmiths next year.

That's great! Her thumbs hover. She swallows the dregs of her coffee. *The thing is, I just haven't been very inspired. As you can see I used to be a sculptor. But it's been a long time since I found a model who inspired me so much. Like a muse, if you know what I mean?*

Nadine reads the message then vanishes again.

She puts her phone face down on the table and tears a hangnail down the length of her thumb, bringing the blood into her mouth. She turns the phone back over. No message. She puts it on airplane mode, locks it, then immediately takes it off airplane mode again. No new messages. But Nadine is online.

What I mean, she writes, *is that as an artist, it is impossible to make work out of nothing. Well, you can. But it means so much to be inspired. We are drawn to people who have something about them. That can be anything. But it has to speak to me, as an artist. That is when the best work is made.*

She sends the paragraph. After four seconds, it shows as being read by Nadine.

That's why I was drawn to you, she continues, *because there is something about you that inspires me. I don't know what. But I can see great images of you in my mind. Really beautiful drawings in charcoal. Large canvases. Drawings and paintings. You are leading me in a new direction.*

Too Much? She presses her thumb quickly, to delete it. But Nadine has already read it. It hangs there: the fact that they are both online. She waiting. Nadine – what?

Then Nadine logs off and she is online, alone.

She pays for the coffee with her credit card.

The hotel restaurant is empty except for two members of staff talking to each other at the bar, one polishing a glass, the other resting their hand on their chin. Ismail nods at her in greeting. You have missed the dinner service, he says.

She pulls herself onto a bar stool and says, I'm not hungry anyway.

This lady, Gustave, I'm telling you. She eats nothing.

She feels very hot and very cold quickly and all at once. She looks up. And Gustave stares back, still polishing a glass. But it is not Gustave. It is someone dressed in the hotel uniform with a gold-coloured name tag with Gustave written on it. Face long and pale. A waiter.

Ismail seems amused. Do you know each other?

No. I just. She rubs her eyes. Know someone with the same name.

Ismail says, So this Gustave, is he dead? You look like you've seen a ghost.

She scans the ornate glassware behind the bar. Unfortunately not, she replies. Unsure why she says this, aside from it being the most obvious joke to make.

She orders and eats a large bowl of mussels, scooping out

the flesh, chewing one-sided, noticing the flavour of the sauce, but other than that they are no different from the mussels on sale in Southend. Gustave glances at her from the other end of the bar, in the way that he would, she knows, with any other guest.

Back in her room, she returns from brushing her teeth to find a missed call from Nadine.

Sorry, she says as soon as the teenager answers the phone. I don't want you to feel forced into anything.

There is a beat before Nadine speaks. I don't, the teenager responds. Voice deeper than she remembers.

Okay. She sighs – relief. But I missed a call from you, she prompts.

Yeah. I was wondering what you want me to do? Like, if I modelled for you.

Anything you want, she says, too quickly again. We can—

Like a nude?

Thrown out like a burr, it sticks. She stops, struck. Is that. Is that what you're worried about?

Because you're talking about drawings and paintings. I just want to know what's expected of me. Like, how much time? Because I am preparing for my exams.

Nadine is Nadine: both child and adult.

She suggests they do an initial drawing session – some brief studies with pencil. To get a feel for things. Maybe she could even offer drawing lessons, if she's interested?

No, Nadine says.

Okay. But I can work around you. I'm free whenever.

In the mini fridge there is beer, a small bottle of champagne, bottled water. She drinks the champagne. Opens the beer and sips it intermittently. She hates beer. The television, muted, glows in the dark. She watches as someone falls down a set of stairs. She begins to drift off against the crushed velvet headboard, but then is alerted awake by her phone vibrating against the beer bottle still clutched in her hand.

Tomorrow after school?

It is a warm afternoon. She returns to the sculpture in the park: the woman cast onto her side, swept by something, arms up to it, a defence or a submission? A strength in the body despite this. Nadine naming it. La Rivière. An artwork they both know.

An hour later, Nadine arrives. Man, if my friends knew I was doing this, they'd go crazy.

It's your face that I want, she tells Nadine, directing her to sit on the grass beside the lake. Nadine pulls absent-mindedly at a white trainer sock, having removed her shoes soon after settling. The teenager is dappled by the sun as it passes through a willow tree. It is not hard to translate the heart of her chin to paper, her snub nose, the heavy scoop of her eye sockets. It surprises her to find she is immersed. But Nadine appears to have difficulty sitting still, lips pursing, eyebrows moving, flicking back her hair or pinching a bug from her mouth, laughing. There is a mole at the base of her neck. She begins talking nervously, words spilling over themselves, to fill the silence.

So you live in London, right? Wow, an artist living in London. That is so cool. Nadine brushes her hair back with a flat palm. I love art so much. Especially the Pre-Raphaelites. I have so many books about the artists. Their lives are just so interesting. I've already decided I want to study art history at university.

Oh really?

Yes. But… Nadine becomes still briefly, closes off again, looking into the middle distance. What did your parents think about you being an artist?

It was never really a conversation we had.

Nadine nods once. Pulls at her jumper sleeve.

She stops drawing, pencil point hanging over the page. What do your parents say?

Nadine looks at her quickly. Then looks away again, pulling at that sock. I don't know. My parents. Well, more my dad. He doesn't think it will help my career.

The willow tree moves, wind lifting the branches, changing the light on Nadine's face.

What does he do?

Some sales job. He travels. He makes a lot of money.

She sweeps Nadine's jaw in lead, getting it dead right. Do you have a good relationship with him?

Wow, such personal questions.

Sorry, she says.

But Nadine smiles. It's cool. I've always lived with mama but I see him pretty much all the time when he's here. They broke up, like, so long ago, but she still takes his side on everything. Dad knows best, she mimics, shaking her head.

A short silence. She creates Nadine's ear with shadows. The breeze picks up, flicking the ends of Nadine's hair.

But it's not his choice, she says, what you study.

Makes no difference. He says I should do, like, economics, or languages. Communications. And he will be supporting me, you know. So. Nadine's eyes swivel away to a plopping sound from the lake.

She flips to a new page, eyes moving continuously between Nadine and the paper. Lines form quickly, fluidly, with an ease she'd forgotten she possessed.

Sorry, do you mind that I am turning around?

No.

White geese travel in a thick plume along the other bank. Nadine watches them. I love them, she says. The l in love is thick, as though she is pushing over a stone with her tongue. I wish I could draw them. I have tried. Hey, there is something I want to ask. I ask my friend, you know, the one who is going to Goldsmiths? I ask her this all the time, and her friends…

Go ahead.

What made you become an artist?

She now has an almost perfect outline of Nadine's face: turned away, the rise of her cheek, eyes averted. Her pencil hovers above the page. Reapplying it could perfect it further, or ruin it. She sharpens her pencil instead. Your dad is wrong about art history.

Why?

You can do loads with it. You could be a curator or a registrar. You could work in auctioneering. Art sales. Lots of money there. You could be a writer. An academic. A teacher. A researcher.

Now you sound like my dad, Nadine says, and laughs again.

A chunk of lead drops out of the pencil sharpener. A breeze spreads goosebumps along her arm. She sets everything down, then pinches the corner of the page between forefinger and thumb, and tears it out from the sketchbook. She hands the drawing to Nadine, watching the teenager's face brighten as the white of the paper reflects on it, mouth forming a smile.

This is amazing.

She kneels back. The sensation of being on a flat plane, steady for once. Thinking: Can your dad do this?

At a bar several blocks away, Nadine seats herself without hesitation, pulling off her school rucksack and dropping it onto the seat beside her, eyes landing on somebody she recognizes, molars showing in a grin, waving open-handed, her fingers blurring in late-afternoon light. Velvet trimmings, lampshades, dusty curtains. Two middle-aged men, huddled with backs curled like shells. Another person appears at the table and sets down glasses, speaking with Nadine in fluent other-language. The fact of her incomprehension hardens. She is in Nadine's world now.

A coolness slips off the teenager sometime after the second glass. Nadine begins to get louder, voice higher. Her stories are only about her life: her friendship group, teachers, parties.

She has the urge to tell her own anecdotes, but what comes out is only the recounting of things she's seen other people say and do, one-liners from social media. No stories of her own. But it doesn't matter because whatever she says, Nadine leans back in her chair, throws back her head, claps her hands together and laughs. While she waits for Nadine to finish a sprawling saga about a school trip to Germany, she reflects on the contents of her own skull, remembering why she is here. So did your dad remarry? she asks.

Nadine puffs out her cheeks, blowing air through red-dried lips. Uh. Yeah. A few years ago.

What's she like, his new wife?

Uhhhh. Nadine shrugs, fiddles with her empty glass. Yeah. She's cool.

What does she think of you studying art history?

Nadine frowns. It doesn't matter.

Is that because she's an idiot?

Nadine refills her own glass and sets down the bottle. The frown remains. No, she says eventually. No. Just, who cares. Why would she have anything to say about my life.

Across the table, Gustave's eyes are watching her, the square of his face sharper now, shadowed by the dropping sun. What does she think she's doing? She drinks to hide the panic rising in her throat.

Why should I care what my dad's wife thinks?

She feels hot. This was a mistake. She reaches for the bottle. It is empty. I'd better go, she says.

Nadine's tone changes again. What? Why? Where are you going? Aren't you staying in a hotel? Nadine reaches across the table, laying both hands on hers. Oh my god. We should have a party in your room.

Their faces are close. Nadine's fingers are warm and sticky. The thought of more teenagers – specifically more of Nadine's friends staring at her, attractive and suspicious. Her stomach drops.

Nah. I'm not really—

But Nadine is already up, backpack on her shoulder, saying, Come on, let's go.

On the metro Nadine is loud again, talking about another party she went to last weekend and then nothing in particular. She swings herself on a pole, at one point taking her hand and raising it above their heads, laughing.

She pretends not to be embarrassed, looking away, reading adverts. The metro walls are beige. Everyone looks yellow. Nadine gives her a headache. Her cavity begins to throb.

At the hotel, Nadine flumps down on the reception desk in front of Ismail, head on hand, and asks if they can get room serrrrrrviiice, in English but as if exaggerating a French accent. Ismail looks concerned. She loops her arm around Nadine's and pulls her away.

At the lifts she opens her bag and paws through its minimal contents. She does not find what she wants to find. Wait here, she says to Nadine, who straightens into a hammed-up impression of a soldier, arms stiff to her sides.

Ismail is writing in some kind of accounting book.

Have you got any painkillers? I bought some, she says, but

they disappeared. I don't know where. I need surgery on my tooth.

Ismail puts down his pen. You have kidnapped this child from the street?

No, she says, noticing three thick hairs sprouting between his eyebrows. She feels defeated, walks away and sighs loudly, loudly enough for Ismail to know that he should hear it, and that she wants him to hear it. Nadine snaps back into her soldier pose, performs her a salute. She then starts to laugh, the sound bouncing against the walls, echoing up the lift shaft even when the door is closed.

I'm sorry, Nadine says once she has finished laughing, pushing her head against her shoulder. Your face. Your face is just so funny.

She swipes the key card and they step into the room to EDM from Nadine's phone. Without looking behind her she knows that Nadine is pumping a fist. The bed frame squeaks as Nadine hops onto it. She drops her bag beneath the television and goes into the bathroom, locking the door and standing for a moment. She presses her back against the door, sliding all the way until her coccyx hits the tiles, in the way she has seen characters do in films when they are at the point of despair. Tinny phone music spikes through the door.

When she leaves the bathroom, there is something about her expression that causes Nadine to make an apologetic sound and kick the mini fridge door shut with her toe, skinny wrist twisting the cork from a miniature bottle of champagne. She decides not to think about the bill, takes a cigarette from her bag and opens the window, hanging her arm out of the narrow opening. She flicks her cigarette and sparks drift down. A thought of how those sparks drifted into the nothing when she was with Gustave. She considers the smoke alarm on the ceiling, how Gustave had covered it with a blue plastic bag. Where did he get the plastic bag from? What had he purchased to obtain that? Who walks around with a plastic bag?

The EDM track has reached a bridge, a fluid female voice singing in English.

Do you listen to Charlotte Gainsbourg, she tries, shouting.

Nadine does not hear her. She watches the teenager's dancing figure in the window, overlaying the lights outside, a flat plane of Parisian apartments. The music has transitioned into happy hardcore. She realizes she wishes to be elsewhere. Elsewhere meaning nowhere. Nowhere and alone.

Do you want me. Want me to model for you? Nadine is pulling off her jumper, hair rising with static. Throwing the jumper on the floor and beginning to unhook her bra.

She quickly flicks the cigarette out of the window and heads towards Nadine. No. No. Please do not take your clothes off.

Come onnnnnn. There is nothing wrong with it. Flapping her hands away. But just as quickly she appears to lose interest. Hey, are you thinking what I'm thinking?

She does not know what Nadine is thinking. The teenager, not needing an answer, picks up her phone.

For five seconds neither of them says anything.

The music stops because Nadine's phone is ringing.

Oh shit. Nadine's voice, quiet at first. Oh shit, she says again, louder.

What?

I forgot. Shit, shit, shit. Nadine brings the phone to her ear, her staticky hair deflating around a pink flustered face.

Allo?

The room is silent. Then Nadine begins speaking French, a quick, impenetrable French, the words sounding warped and back to front. She watches on with the sense she is no longer a participant in this world: a teenager in a bra stalking around the room, on the phone, somehow draining the champagne bottle without stopping talking. She looks at her own phone in her hand, the background image of the poster from that film that Javier liked so much.

Nadine throws her phone onto the bed. I forgot, she announces. We are having dinner.

Who?

My dad. He is taking me for dinner.

That was your dad on the phone?

Nadine is looking in the mini fridge again. Yes. She opens a can of Heineken. I'm only a little late. He will come get me.

Her stomach plunges. Did you tell him who you were with?

The can is halfway to Nadine's lips. She stops to shrug, saying, I explained the situation.

Did you tell him my name?

What?

Did you tell him my name?

Uh. I think I just said you were my friend. The artist.

Her eyes blur out. Colours come free from their objects and swirl around the room.

When will he be here?

What's wrong?

When will he be here?

I don't know. Like. Fifteen minutes?

Inhaling. Exhaling. Inhaling. Clasping and unclasping her hands. Okay. Okay.

Why are you freaking out?

Why don't you go downstairs now. Wait for him.

Nadine swallows audibly. Now?

You don't want to keep him waiting.

But I said he'd be—

You need to stop drinking.

Why? I'm not drunk.

Yes, you are, she says, but realizes that Nadine is in fact not drunk.

I thought we were both having a good time, no?

She says nothing.

Will you at least come wait with me outside?

Neither of them speak as the lift glides down. She folds her arms, staring at the floor, drawing semicircles with the toes of her elegant flats. Nadine sniffs, brushing back her hair, her jumper too bright, too red, for this space now.

As they leave the lift, Nadine presses the rolled drawing into her hand and wanders off, saying that she needs the bathroom. With the teenager gone, she visualizes running back to her room, leaving Nadine to buzz around, confused, eventually leaving with her father. Instead she finds herself outside, in the warm night, standing among the ornamental plants. What happens now? What does she hope to achieve? Why didn't her tutors ask her what she was doing right then, in the moment? She might have been able to answer that. She needs to get back to her room. She turns to go into the hotel and collides with Nadine. She hands the drawing back to Nadine, dumb.

He won't care that I was modelling, you know, the teenager says, grabbing it.

I'm not worried about that.

So what is it?

At the sight of a car drawing up to the kerb, they both stop and turn to watch. A black saloon with the windows tinted. Here he is. What car had she imagined him driving? None, actually. The fantasies were built upon holding hands in parks, cycling down cobbled streets together to buy bread and put it in their wicker baskets, the beach. It seems obvious now that he would drive something which looks like an Uber X, which is now aligning itself with the kerb. A small feeling emerges: she does not want to lose Nadine now.

The driver's door opens. A man steps out, dressed in a black suit. It is not Gustave. The driver is opening the rear passenger door. Two women are climbing out, dressed in *LBDs*.

You know, you are right. Nadine appears to have forgotten her previous line of questioning. I am going to tell my dad I'm going to study art history.

The car drives away and the two women walk down the pavement.

I'll tell him I got advice from a real artist. And he will just have to deal with it.

I'm not a real artist.

Nadine clicks her tongue and unrolls the drawing, holding it at arm's length for them both to see. She has caught it all: the glow of Nadine's forehead, the gentle turn of her neck, Gustave's eyes.

How can you tell me you are not a real artist?

The blood flows hot around her body. Nadine does not need an answer because she believes what she has been told. Nadine trusts her.

I have to go. Go and. Go do something. You'll be all right waiting here, won't you?

Nadine drapes her long arms over her, pulls her in. The feeling of her jumper rubs against her chin. Nadine is fruit-scented and saying something about seeing her again soon.

She stands at the far edge of the hotel restaurant window and looks out. She watches Nadine shrug, bite her sleeve, fold her arms, lean on one leg. A small and slightly dusty silver car pulls up. Nadine walks around its front and opens the passenger door. The street lights reflected in the windscreen darken and obscure the interior of the car. She bites down and dares the pain of her cavity to overwhelm her.

The overcrowding at the Louvre fills the foyer with hot damp air. She stands at the ticket desk, where a woman scrutinizes the difference between the ticket on her phone and her face. The ticket is admission for eighteen- to twenty-five-year-olds. The woman peers at her a final time, then makes a minute side movement with her head to confirm that she is permitted entry.

She has to dodge around gathered groups and wandering couples, all taking up space and moving too slowly. Each new room appears busier than the last, and she speeds up, moving straight on, seeing nothing and regretting her visit. Eventually the rooms become smaller, less full, the air cooler. Obviously ancient objects in glass display cases. She bends to look more closely at one cabinet, which contains small things and parts of things. The placard says: Fragments of statues and bases damaged by Akkadian armies during the sack and burning of the city about 2300 BC, but the information passes straight through the front of her skull and out the other side. She is unable to take in the information. Which armies? Which city? Which burning? On a shelf beneath there is an arrangement of disembodied feet, uniformly snapped from the ankle. Then an assortment of other miniature body parts, broken off. Her forehead touches the cool glass. There is what first appears to be a length of bone, before she makes out the shape of carved thumbs and fingers. A hand, broken at the wrist, shaped in a way to suggest it is holding another.

As she pushes up from her knees to stand, she experiences a head rush. What is it all for, she wonders, this collection of objects, this mass preservation of things. Surely it is not for these people reflected in the glass. Who is really interested in a broken bit of bone? She feels the warmth of a presence beside her: Nadine, sweating, pushing her hair back, apologizing, laughing and explaining she is late because of something, a story to do with her friends and a weird person on the Metro. Eventually Nadine stops talking and notices her surroundings. What are you doing in here? This is all just broken things.

She crouches again and gestures. Look at this one. Presses her finger against the glass. This is supposed to be two hands, but we see only one. The hands are joined, but the second one is only there by way of suggestion, by its absence, by way of negative space.

Nadine brings her face nearer to the display case. Then her attention is carried off by something else. Oh, look at all these tiny feet!

After wandering up a small staircase, they approach a plaster body and come to a synchronized stop.

You know, your sculpture from your degree show. It was not what I expected.

She leads them into another room. What did you expect?

I don't know. Something that looked like a human.

She and Jenny had started talking to each other, forming what she supposed was a friendship after the first six months of their art A level at college in Southend, when it appeared that they were both making small-scale figurative sculptures. Over time, her own work developed, becoming amorphous, bodied but blob-like, anti-aesthetic she called it. But Jenny continued to make the same thing continuously: the figurines. They're just people. You're just making models of people, she once said to Jenny, unable to keep it to herself any more. You're not doing anything with it. In the class's critique sessions she would re-lentlessly pick apart other students' work, leaving them looking despondent, fed up, wishing they had never picked art. In turn, she would dismiss the class's criticisms of her own work with ease, and so they soon shut up. Whatever she had to say about Jenny's artwork, however, seemed to wash over her. Jenny had nothing to say beyond expressing which types of people she was planning to make next: ones in hijabs, for example. It was something about the way Jenny looked at her, a way which felt knowing, knowingly about her, because outside of the college walls she had nothing to say about anything.

Only when Nadine prompts, What happened then? does she realize she has been saying this out loud.

She swallows, scratches her face, thinking vaguely of the painting they are passing, exhibited by virtue of its oldness. After their A-level exams, she messaged Jenny to say she had got an A★ grade, to which Jenny responded that she, too, got an A★. She started declining Jenny's invitations to go out. In the months before she moved to London to study at the Slade, Jenny messaged her to say she had sold a figurine at some charity sale for amateur artists. She did not respond. Later on, Jenny started posting on social media every time she made a sale, every time she had a group exhibition in a local gallery and then a solo exhibition in the only commercial gallery in Southend. The work never changed. Jenny sent her invitations to all the private views. She did not respond.

And now she makes these stupid little sculptures for a living, she concludes.

I mean to you. What happened to you?

It is difficult to identify what happened. She reaches into her memory, finding its soft base. At the Slade no one was persuad-ed by what she said about her work. The students were quicker and more exacting with criticism than at college, saying things she sometimes did not understand. She stayed up until the early hours researching art manifestos, learning phrases from critical theory. Rehearsing her lines. But deploying these only seemed to bring more criticism. It appeared that she did not understand what she was saying at all. Can these things really be anti-aesthetic, an American student had asked, when these are essentially just nice-looking objects? But it's the abjectness, she responded, the abjectness I'm going for, there's no aesthetic to that. She remembers how the tutor's head snapped towards her at this, attention piqued. Ah, but, the tutor said, if you're saying that you intend to capture the essence of the human form, which I agree is in many respects abject, what you're really doing with these works is attesting to some kind of inherent beauty to this essence, which is a rather romantic view. Is this what you believe? Some of the students, including the American, had glanced at each other and laughed quietly. Her brain emptied. Romantic? Surely to be romantic would mean to be entirely non-conceptual. Maybe her work was – even worse – basic. Commercial. This fear bore down on her for the rest of the day, on her way to the bus stop, on the crowded and damp bus back to her houseshare. Romantic?

After that, she resolved to say nothing about her work at all. The objects lost their bodies, moving beyond suggestions of limb to total abstraction, formed from everyday debris, litter from the studio floor. And as she said nothing about her work, the other students had less and less to say. This exasperated the tutors and caused eye-rolling among the other students. But nobody could know more than her if they did not know what she knew.

The sculpture at her degree show was the last thing she ever made. While other students fiddled with their work, paying precise attention to wall fittings, she kicked her sculpture into its allotted space and left. By then she had already stopped calling herself an artist.

Nadine continues looking at her long after she has finished speaking. That's so sad, she says.

She wonders if Nadine understands at all. Feeling self-conscious, she pretends to be interested in a painting of two high-society children in a garden, switching off her memory like a light. Behind them is a stream of people heading towards the Mona Lisa.

They climb more stairs and enter an exhibit where the walls are dove grey. Natural light seeps through from the skylight. They are the only people here. They pass through room to room of peinture française, room to room of eyes gazing back from refinement and estates. Without the press of bodies around them, they feel able to slow down. Nadine stops at a painting of a monkey in a dressing gown. She watches how the teenager turns to look at her, smiling, and notices that her face changes in response, smiling back. A wordless acknowledgement between them, the ridiculousness of the art. It feels like relief. A monkey in a dressing gown.

Towards the end of the exhibit they stop before a portrait of three figures: two women and a man. The man is angled to face them, half-reclining. There is a marked difference in age between the two women. The younger woman, perhaps the daughter, is looking up, sheet music pinched between her fingers, mind elsewhere, maybe just about to sing. The elder woman, who she presumes is the man's wife, gazes at him. At his side lies a dead bird. In the wife's gaze there is an undercurrent which the youngest appears unaware of, talking or singing over it. In the darkest point of the painting, in the centre, there is the eye of a dog. The animal's jaw is obscured by the man's hand. On the other side, as though an extension of the dog's face, there is a gun: the slim blackness rests in the crook of the man's elbow, pointed over his shoulder. The man's insouciant expression remains.

Nadine raises a finger to the painting, towards the dead bird then stops, seeming to remember not to touch. This can have different meanings, she says. But I can't work it out.

Like what?

Like. Nadine chews her jumper sleeve. Sometimes this is a symbol for wealth, or satisfaction. Because it has been hunted. But also, because it is dead, sometimes it is just a symbol of mortality. That these things will come to an end.

What things?

Nadine shrugs, wiping her chewed wet sleeve on her front. Everything, she says.

This is wrong, she thinks. It never ends. The lavishly dressed daughter is a symbol for the man's wealth. His lineage.

Does your dad know you're with me?

Huh. Nadine shrugs again, touching her hair, affectedly casual. No. I, erm. I skipped school to be here. So I can't tell my parents. She puts a hand on her stomach. Hey, I'm hungry.

At McDonald's Nadine selects things from an electronic screen, index finger anointing items quickly. A burger. Fries. A drink. Removing that one. Selecting another drink. Sauce – three pots in red.

Your turn.

A memory: her mum's hand around her own small one. Bright lights, delicious smells, but unable to enter, unable to afford. Shouldn't eat it anyway, her mum was saying. Too un-healthy, fattening, full of additives. It was always like this, despite the margarine and white bread they ate at home. Except for once, when she was five or six. A treat, her mum had said. She remembers the heat seeping through the cardboard box, opening and unwrapping, excited to find the toy at the bottom. She remembers that she was not thinking, moving too quickly and knocking the box on the floor with her elbow. It all fell out, the burger hitting the tiles, fries and innards spilling out. Everything ruined. Stupid.

She presses a picture of fries.

That's it? You're just having fries?

It's all I want.

That's so boring.

But it's expensive.

What? You cannot just eat fries. Nadine's arm brushes her shoulder, her finger scrolling through the menu, selecting a picture of a burger. If you order a meal, it is—

Okay. Okay. Her own hand meets Nadine's at the screen, batting it away. The taste is in her mouth already, the grease, the fat, the meat, the animal, the abattoir. Nausea. Another memory: the first year of her art degree, when everyone was still working out who everyone else was. At McDonald's she sat and watched, not ordering anything, watching how everyone became the same in there, all eating the same shit. I can't afford it, she'd say. I can't afford it. Surely you can afford just a milkshake, nuggets, fries, something – they're only 99p. And she'd shrug, buckle down. Nope. Don't want anything anyway. Not hungry.

The sound of her card being declined. She puts away her credit card and tries her debit card, already knowing the answer, seeing it scroll across the digital screen.

Declined.

Don't worry, I'll get it.

Nadine's tone hints at – it is too awful to acknowledge – pity.

When Nadine taps her card on the pad, she notices Nadine's fingernails, a consistent yellow-pink, without scratches of vitamin deficiency, almond-shaped and strong. She swallows her sudden hatred. For Nadine, for herself, for everyone. The machine says Approuvé. Almost obscured by Nadine's thumb, the card says M. G CARON.

At a table by the window, Nadine dips a chicken nugget into a pot of sauce and says, I don't understand why you stopped making art.

I told you.

You told me that you stopped making art. Not why.

Someone wearing a beret passes by the window. Her burger sits unwrapped.

Because I couldn't afford to.

You could not just make money from your art? Your friend—

Yeah, my friend makes art which just sells and that's all it does.

That's not a good thing?

It's not what I want.

But if you want to make art and live, it has to sell, no?

Another person in a beret passes. She considers excusing herself to go to the bathroom, visualizes sliding off her stool and walking there, then what would she do? Stand in a cubicle and wait for this heavy feeling to pass. Stay in there until her existence became a zero, nothing, forgotten. Everything wiped clean.

…like, they dedicated their life to it, you know?

What?

I was just saying. Nadine pinches fries. Like, the artists we see in the Louvre. They dedicated their life to art. That's what it takes.

She stares at a lick of ketchup and a crumb on Nadine's lip. You know nothing about art.

The teenager pauses briefly before eating more chips. Why do you say that?

Because life was completely different back then. You could live in poverty in those days. You can't now.

Nadine's face is blank, which is more annoying. Is the struggle not part of it? Because then you get the pay-off.

What is the pay-off, she asks, knowing her voice is pointed. Why should I struggle. How many artists do you think found success? It's all posthumous. Only in death, she says, seeing Nadine's brief look of confusion.

Greatness, Nadine responds, mouth full of fries.

But what is that? What is greatness?

Think about it, Nadine says. You get to live forever.

How many of these artists even lived long enough to benefit from any greatness? And anyway it's easy for you to say all this. You've got your dad to support you.

So?

If you have money, you have time. And time is freedom because you can do whatever the fuck you want without having to worry about surviving. If you have to worry about surviving then you can't wait around for someone to notice you, to buy your work. You have to get the income from somewhere. That's what I had to do. I had to get a job. And that left me without time. So what is the fucking point?

Nadine chews, then looks away. Swallows. Eventually says that, honestly, she'd rather she didn't have money. Because the money means that papa decides what I do.

Oh really, Nadine, is that your biggest problem. She slides off her stool. Honestly. You don't know how lucky you are.

She walks across the McDonald's, towards a corner, then follows a corridor down towards a door without markings, assuming the toilets are here. She pulls it open and walks down a set of stairs, the wall tiles changing from white to black, down to where her footsteps are audible, heavy, slap–slap–slap against the new quiet. At the bottom there is a new smell, damp, mossy, old dishwater. Someone in a grey McDonald's uniform appears from behind a corner and says something in French, at which point she turns and goes back up the steps, slap–slap–slap, through the door down the corridor, returning to where Nadine sits facing the window, the back of her head appearing vulnerable, pitiful, having been left sitting on her own, eating fries.

She lays one hand on the edge of the table, apprehensive, unsure whether to sit. An uneasy water is between them now. Nadine continues chewing slowly but fervently at the same time, like a calf. Another person wearing a beret passes the window.

What do you think of people who wear berets?

Nadine says nothing and so she keeps talking.

They're trying so hard to look French. It's obvious they're not from here. Real French people don't actually wear berets.

The teenager shrugs.

What do you think, she says again.

Nadine is obviously not interested. About what?

People who pretend to be French.

People pretend to be French?

Well. Yeah. You know. People who wear berets and red lipstick, wear black and white, monochrome and all that. They're pretending to look – to be, to be French. French girl make-up is a red lip, isn't it? French girls love a red lip. And their skincare too. They're, like, religious about it, aren't they? It's more important than make-up. That's what these people don't understand. They think putting on red lipstick makes them French. But they look overdone. And that's the problem. They look so superficial. When the key to it is confidence, isn't it. French girls are confident naturally, aren't they. They don't overthink these things. They don't eat McDonald's. Well, I mean they do. They eat what they want, but they're always slim. Right? It's because they drink black coffee and smoke. And it's also just the way that they are. And they look good effortlessly. Nonchalantly. You can't pretend to be French. You can't pretend to be French.

Nadine does not respond at first. Mouth beaking to drink from her straw. The sound of the empty paper cup rising up through the ice. Eventually she says, I don't know. It's all marketing I guess. No one, like, thinks they are French if they're not. It's just an idea.

But it also is a real thing, being a French girl. The idea doesn't just come from anywhere. Like you. You're a French girl.

Me?

She sits down. Like how you dress is so easy, so laid-back, and you look. Just. Complete. And you don't even wear make-up. You don't need to, because you're confident. Your confidence comes naturally. You might wear a little bit of make-up but it's just to enhance your features, right? You haven't even done anything to your eyebrows. And your nails aren't painted. And you shrug and you don't care and you're just so. That's so French, Nadine. That's you.

Nadine pushes two fries into her mouth, where the blunt ends dance between her teeth. That's rude. I have my eyebrows shaped.

The table surface is sticky and grips her palm. Sorry, she says.

Nadine shrugs, unaware of the irony. Also, I am wearing a, how is it called? Tinted moisturizer. Picks up the remains of her burger then drops it, uninterested. It falls apart against its paper wrapping. Honestly I have never thought about these things.

She picks up a fry, chews it too quickly, too late before her tongue can move it to the other side of her mouth: the heat sits in her rotten back tooth. She reaches for her drink but the ice cold makes it worse. She taps her foot against the stool, to override the pain with a new sensation. Let's swap places, she manages.

Swap places, Nadine responds flatly.

Yeah. You can pretend to be me. Then you can be poor. And I'll be you, and then I can have your dad and make him do whatever I want.

Nadine grins briefly, and it is difficult to know what this is precisely in response to. I think you would kill each other, she says.

Ismail is standing outside the hotel, head bent, appearing to be in deep conversation with a woman she recognizes as the receptionist who was here when she first arrived at this hotel. The woman's arms are folded and she is wearing a blazer, and black high heels which make her taller than Ismail.

She walks back a few paces, waits, counts, one two three four five six seven eight nine ten. Now Ismail is alone, hands in his pockets, kicking at something. He looks up momentarily on her approach, and then again when he realizes it is her.

She stops in the same place as the woman and folds her arms. I've run out of money. I don't have any more money to eat or to stay here. And my prepaid booking runs out on Sunday.

Oh, he says, squinting against the low sun behind her.

She stares at the hairs between his eyebrows. I want to stay here. In Paris, I mean. Even if I wanted to go back to England, I don't even have money to get back. My ticket was one-way. What should I do? If I could just, I don't know, have my booking extended. Then I can get everything sorted. And then I can just pay you back. The hotel, I mean.

He scratches his head. Listen, I am busy right now. His eyes flash in the direction of the hotel entrance and back to her. We can… talk later?

Come to my room, she says.

His face shows no outward change. Sure, he responds.

There is a white paper bag next to her on the bed, which Ismail has placed there before retreating across the room, leaning casually against the desk, hands in his pockets again. It is another filled croissant, unfortunately, he says. We have too many left over.

What were you talking about with that woman earlier?

That's my boss, he says. I'm always in trouble with her. His skin is more sallow than usual, the hollows around his eyes darker. He brings a hand out of his pocket and taps his fingers absently on the desk before lifting the cover of her sketchbook. Flicking through the sheets. Stopping. Pressing a finger onto a page.

This is the girl, he says. The girl you were with the other night.

She stares at the back of his neck, black hair climbing up from beneath the shirt collar. He turns another page then looks at her, mouth pulled up at one side.

You're very good at this, he says.

She pushes herself up off the bed, walks across to him at the desk, placing her hand on the sketchbook, so that their fingers are near. Is there anything you can do to help me?

His eyelashes flick, registering her nearness. You mean. Another croissant?

The joke annoys her. She moves her leg closer to his. Ismail, she says.

He pulls back his head, creating distance between their faces, clearing his throat behind his fist. She catches the sour end of his breath.

The thing is. She repositions her weight. Brings her hand close to his, fingers touching now. I've noticed that you've been paying me a lot of attention. Ever since I got here. I know what it means. She rests her little finger upon his thumb. He is avoiding her gaze, looking at the sketchbook. She takes his name badge in her other hand, wrapping her fingertips around it. This makes him flinch. I could stay with you, couldn't I?

His voice is quiet as he brings out his thumb from under her finger. I'm sorry, but I cannot do any more for you.

What?

And this – he politely unpicks her other hand from his name badge – is inappropriate behaviour.

But you've been all over me since I got here.

Ismail sighs loudly. I think you have misunderstood the situation.

The feeling is the same: of being cast onto the floor by Gustave, being told she has misunderstood.

Is this what men have decided I'm good for? Leading me on then saying it's all in my head.

Sorry, leading you on? What does this mean?

Why have you been helping me?

It is my job, he says.

No. No, you're lying. It's not in your job description to give me free food, is it? She casts her arm over the room. Not to come into my room and chat with me. Is it.

Ismail freezes momentarily and then says, I have been helping you because I can see that you need it.

Her mouth falls open. I don't need your help.

And you invited me to your room. Look, I am not here to argue with you. I am just a friendly guy, okay. He moves over to the door and places his hand on the door handle.

Okay, fine. Go and bother someone else.

He pauses. Opens the door but then closes it. Looks at her again. If it helps, he says, you have been one of my favourite guests.

Shut up.

Okay, he says.

Fuck off, she says. She picks up the white bag with the croissant inside and casts it across the room. But Ismail is already gone and so the package hits the door and slides down. She stares, fingers clenching and unclenching, before diving after it, unsheathing the croissant and stuffing it in her mouth.

There is black-red blood in the toilet bowl, a clot of it clinging to the side. Taking a wad of toilet paper and wrapping it around her fingers, she places it in her underwear. The poverty of it makes the feeling worse. Floating somewhere behind her head is the image of her with Gustave's baby, wearing a dress which is blue, no, yellow. Red. Not red. The image disappears through the wall.

Outside her room people travel in sounds – children's voices, suitcases, unknown languages – towards the lifts, towards the breakfast buffet, which is eighteen euros and ninety-five cents extra. A dull ache grows at the base of her stomach and beyond it. Menstruation or hunger, the pain is the same. At least she will lose weight.

She turns on France 24. There is the woman with the pearl earrings. She turns it off, deciding to take a walk and to walk until she is numb. As she steps out of the hotel room, her foot slips from under her. She looks down. On the floor there is a tray with another croissant for her.

In the afternoon she calls Nadine, who does not answer but rings back immediately afterwards with a video request. There is a small inset in the corner, reflecting her own face back, and she looks vile. Oily, tired. She repositions the phone but no angle is flattering.

Nadine flips her phone camera to show brief, blurred footage of what look like textbooks. I am doing my homework, she says. When the camera returns to its original position, Nadine's face appears blocky, unrendered. Nose made slenderer.

If you're busy then I can go.

No, no.

Nadine looks at her, although by the position of her eyes she is more likely looking at her own image.

I can talk.

Alright, she responds, and then has nothing to say.

Nadine props her phone against something and continues working. The image pixelates, then becomes clearer, and she watches Nadine writing with her right hand.

What's up, Nadine says eventually.

Just. Just wanted to say hello.

Oh. Hello.

Do you still like me?

Huh?

She scrunches her face, covering her eyes with her hand, keeping it there. It's alright, you're busy. I'll just go.

Why do you ask?

She sighs through her nose, eyes still covered. I feel like you might not like me.

Why?

Because of yesterday. The things I said. She peeks through her fingers, watching as the teenager sets down her pen, apparently thinking for a few seconds.

I still like you, Nadine says. But just. Yeah. You were being strange. I did not understand what it was all about.

Right. She nods to herself. Right. I know. There is a stinging sensation at the top of her nose.

Why are you covering your face?

No reason.

I mean, that whole French girl thing, Nadine continues. It's just a stupid idea, you know? Like, a hashtag. I don't wake up and think about these things. Nadine closes the textbook. I'm just. I'm just me, you know?

Yeah. She presses away the sting, eyes wet. Sorry.

Hey, also, you reminded me that I need to get a manicure. So later I am going with my friend. Do you want to come?

I can't afford it, she replies, and realizes this is a relief.

Oh yeah. You have no money at all. A classic penniless artist. Nadine adjusts her position, bringing up a leg and bending it beneath herself, knocking over her phone in the process. She looks at her own image once more then puts down her phone on the bed. Now both phones are looking at ceilings.

I'm penniless, she says, but artists make art. And I'm not making any art at all.

Yeah you are, Nadine's voice responds.

Maybe I don't even want to be an artist any more.

Why not?

I don't know. I just can't see it. It doesn't seem real.

So, what then?

She thinks of saying, Do I have to know? But images are forming in her mind, rooted in her stomach: the mirage of herself holding the baby, wearing the dress. The image is incomplete without Gustave. I think I want to have a baby.

What did you say? A baby? The sound of something made of glass meeting wood rings out from Nadine's world. Really? Is that all you want? I'm just. You could do so many other things. You live in London, you went to the Slade. You could do so much more with your life. If all you want to do is have a baby. Then, I don't know. What does that make you?

A mother, she responds. Her chest is tight. But not just like that. I want someone to choose me. To choose me to have their baby. I want to be chosen.

Another pause before Nadine's palm appears on the screen, righting her phone position. That's a weird thing to say.

Is it?

Hey, where are you? She watches Nadine's face come back into shot.

I'm here, she says.

I can't see you. I think you knocked yours over?

She does nothing.

Nadine is looking into the screen – really looking. Are you still there?

Yes.

Can you, uh, come back on screen—

No.

Alright. Nadine sits back, chewing a lip. But what you said just now is weird.

How is it weird?

Surely you should be choosing who to have a baby with, no? Not the other way around. It feels creepy.

Her hand is moving across the duvet to pick up the phone, to end the call.

Sorry, Nadine says, and her hand stops, fingers around the phone without taking further action. I am just surprised. I did not expect you to say something like that. It's just you do not seem, uh, what is the word? Like someone who would want a baby. Motherly. You don't seem that way.

Nadine. Don't get your nails done.

What?

Don't get your nails done. You don't need it.

Another short laugh. What? That's ridiculous. I know I don't need it. I want it. I saw these really cool nails on Instagram, they have like a little heart shape on the end? I'll show you.

No, don't. It's fine. I'm going now. Lifting the phone, she catches Nadine's expression, mouth open in a small O, preparing to speak. Then she closes her mouth and looks directly at her. Big eyes steady. All right. Show me the nails.

Nadine flips the camera to show her an image on her MacBook. In the photo there are two hands, one laid upon the other. Fingers splayed to show the nails on both. The design is almond-shaped, clear, with the two curves of a heart at the base of the nail. On the little finger, there is a tiny red heart, floating. Creepy, she thinks. What is the difference between creepy and romantic? She splays out her own fingers, imagining red hearts there.

After the call ends, she gets up to make coffee, standing to watch the small kettle boil, beginning to shake, the water bubbling until the switch clicks off. When she pours it, only a few drops come out, then steam, which catches her finger. It burns. Idiot. She replaces the kettle and brings the burn to her mouth. Idiot. Idiot. Idiot. The finger in her mouth gets bitten, teeth around it. Idiot. Idiot. Idiot. She bites harder, would keep biting, except her phone has started vibrating on the bed. Idiot. She wants to become something or become nothing at all. Nadine is calling her again. Hand in mouth, she does not answer. A few seconds later there is a message asking her if she wants to come for dinner tomorrow, at her house.

She messages back: *Who will be there?*

Me. Please come.

Nadine has told her that she lives with her mother. The woman Gustave chose first of all – before Christine, before her. A woman obscured by the blank spot in her knowledge. Then Nadine sends her a photo. It is her drawing of Nadine by the lake in the park, framed on her bedroom wall. Perhaps there is kinship to be found in Nadine's mother. And what else could be found in that? A spare room? The burnt patch of skin on her finger is angry and tender.

She pretends she's not going, but she knows she is. Her stomach is bloated. Feels like a sack of stones. She stands sideways to the mirror. Bloat like early pregnancy. She feels disgusting. She applies a second layer of moisturizer, red lipstick.

Nadine stands at the top of the steps of the metro station and embraces her. Ribs compress in the hug. Over Nadine's shoulder she sees a rusted metal frame: an old market stall, abandoned. There is a chill breeze. She breaks the embrace first. Look! Nadine says, holding out her hands to show her nails are adorned with little hearts.

They walk down an avenue and Nadine talks non-stop. And I was like, if you don't even know the curriculum, how are you supposed to be prepared. Right? But it went on for so long. Then I was just like, you know what, this is stupid. So I got out the booklet and showed her and she was just like, Oh.

The teenager leads her to a building with a windowless front and single metal door. Inside, the lobby is larger and brighter, with marbled floors and a large plant in the middle all lit by a skylight. The smell of a new conversion, cement freshly settled. Nadine's mother is beginning to take shape in her mind – she has nicer hair than she has previously imagined.

What's your mum's name again?

My mom?

They head up wide marble steps. The thickness of the walls shuts out the world. No sound except for their footsteps. They pass a large, framed abstract painting, spatters of red and yellow, and come to a landing where there are two doors. Nadine stops outside one and presses the doorbell.

A click and a gush of new air. And then – a solar eclipse. In a turtleneck. Frenchman style. The stones in her stomach roll. That face betraying nothing. Except there: the nostril flare.

Nadine is talking, the words swimming.

Gustave stares at her.

She glances back at the stairwell. Considers running. Then looks back at Gustave.

He opens his mouth to speak. This is it.

The vibration of his voice moves through her before she understands the words.

Nice to meet you.

He bends at the waist, and his face nears hers. Her fists are tight balls. He presses the side of his face to hers, a silent kiss. Moves to her other cheek. When the greeting is complete, his black eyes lock onto hers.

She watches Nadine greet her father the same way, air kiss to air kiss. From behind either side of the teenager's head, Gustave's eyes still do not leave hers. A warning. Then the teenager is swallowed up by the hallway, loudly saying that she is going to get changed and that she is very hungry.

They are alone together. Gustave's gaze chills her. She fastens her hands behind her back, hiding telltale trembling, regretting not making more of an effort with her outfit.

So, he says, turning to block the hallway down which Nadine has disappeared. You're here. In my home.

Her tongue is dry, her body spiking with fear. The seconds stretch. The corner of his mouth twitches.

When Gustave speaks again, it is in a whisper. Do not bring her into this.

Nadine calls out, in French. Her father ignores her.

I have no idea how this has happened, but I am giving you a chance to leave. Now.

She loosens her hands, letting them swing by her sides. Straightens her shoulders, registers the click of her joints. Sniffs. Excuse me, she says, approaching Gustave. She comes level to his chest, remaining there briefly, before passing under his gaze into the yellow light of his home. His presence beats behind her.

The interior is large, open-plan. A kitchen and lounge area. There are huge French windows, the city beyond, vast and like a painting, slate roofs, attic windows, balconies. She finds herself searching for the Eiffel Tower. It is apparently not included in this view. This is strangely satisfying.

Glass meets granite. Nadine is back, taking out wine glasses from a kitchen cabinet and placing them on the worktop. Three lined up together.

I thought you lived with your mum?

The teenager glances at her, too-long jumper sleeve wrapped around the neck of a bottle of red wine, the cork half out, having given up on a corkscrew. His house, my house, she shrugs. Inserting the cork into her mouth, teeth pulling to release it.

Yes, and you have your own door key, non? You do not need to summon me. Gustave has joined them. He reaches between them and grips the bottle, taking it from Nadine's grasp.

Nadine rolls her eyes and declares with faux dramatics, I forgot. Glancing at her fingernails, she startles. Oh no! My nail. Shit. Papa, it came off.

It is difficult to concentrate on anything. Her vision begins to smudge, everything becoming wet paint, then wet nothing. Gustave's form has moved across the kitchen and is speaking in French now. Pulling at a cupboard door to reveal a wine rack, replacing Nadine's bottle and returning with a different bottle in his hand, held lengthways as though he is a sommelier. You have brought a special guest, he says. So we will drink this special wine.

Her vision returns and the bottle becomes solid. White wine. She hates white wine. It is as if he knows.

Nadine is picking at her ruined fingernail. He thinks he is a wine expert, she grumbles.

Gustave unleashes the cork with an expert's flair. He fills one of the glasses. Nadine takes it with both hands and drinks. Gustave fills the other two glasses and hands one to her without looking at her. The stem. You must hold it by the stem.

She takes it by the stem automatically, then realizes he was instructing Nadine, who is pulling a sulky face but now doing so. Gustave sets down the bottle and holds his own glass briefly to his chest. Santé, he says. Now he is swigging as though to swallow the entire glass, but bringing it down from his face, it appears he has drunk almost nothing. She shivers once, violently, involuntarily.

What was it you said, papa? About the drawing she did of me. Nadine brings up her hand to enunciate. You said, It has really captured me.

Ah, well. You are my beautiful daughter. Gustave brings his arm swooping around Nadine's shoulders, pulling her in to him. Nobody can capture you perfectly.

For a moment in their embrace they look identical.

Nadine rolls her eyes again, flushed, and pulls away, smoothing her hair with a sleeve. She turns to her, saying they should go out onto the balcony.

She watches Gustave. He watches Nadine. Why don't you go and collect dinner, he says to his daughter. I ordered from our favourite place.

What. Why do I have to go? He's an old man who likes to order by calling the restaurant, Nadine explains to her now, picking up her wine again. And then he likes to waste more time by saying he will collect it. Then back to her father. Why can't you just order Deliveroo like everyone else?

Standing witness to father and daughter, polite smile sustaining, she feels like a scarecrow in a burning field.

Gustave prises Nadine's drink back from her mouth by the stem. Also I would like some time to talk with your friend. To get to know her.

She sees the light trapped within the wine glasses, the crystalline pattern on the worktop, the relief of the sky through those large windows and the network of streets she imagines running beneath it.

I could come with— she starts, but Nadine and Gustave are already fussing over something in French. Gustave has taken out a wallet and is handing the teenager a few euro notes. They prefer cash, he says to her.

The statement hovers. She goes to nod in response, a conversational instinct, then stops. He has not looked at or spoken to her directly since she arrived.

Hey. Nadine is nudging her and winking as she heads out of the kitchen. I think he likes you.

Her forearm jolts, hand preparing to latch onto Nadine, with the urge to say, Let me come with you, please. She wants out. But to do so would mean Gustave has won, and so she withdraws her hand. Now she and Gustave are watching Nadine leave, down the corridor and out of the apartment. There is the sound of the door closing.

Gustave spins, swift and measured, and walks across the kitchen to where he had stood before. There are two metres between them. He picks up the wine bottle and refills his glass. He puts down the bottle and folds his arms, turning his head to address the window and not her. So. Will you tell me what you are doing here?

Her chest hurts. She drains her glass and says nothing. Without Nadine present, the apartment is silent. No sound leaking in from the outside world.

Gustave sniffs and continues. Okay. I will tell you what I think. You are upset because you expected more from me. Which is, honestly, ridiculous. As I gave you no impression that there would be anything further between us. I can forgive you for this, however. It is a common misconception by women. He stops, for caution or effect. Jaw set. She sees the whites of his eyes. But then you show up at my office, tell the receptionist that you are my wife, and cause a scene. This makes me believe that you are delusional.

He turns at the waist to pick up his glass. He does not drink from it, instead he holds it before him, twirling it so that it glints in the light as he admires it.

And then I am informed that you have made certain allegations. I trust that you know how these things can threaten a man's livelihood. His career, personal life, his reputation.

Impulsively her free thumb moves into her palm, for the skin to be picked. She retracts it. Considers whether to say that Oscar was not supposed to tell him because that was not the point.

Naturally, Gustave continues, these allegations are false, and that can be proven. I have consulted with my lawyer and I have no concerns if you were to proceed. However, this made me think that perhaps what you want is money. This is something I would be willing to negotiate.

For a few beats he is silent. She waits.

But then you befriend my daughter. Gustave sets down his glass with a determinedly casual movement. And now I am concerned. About how to proceed. Because apparently you have information about me and my family. And you appear to be using this information to get to me. And now I really do not know what your objective is. Could you tell my daughter things about me, I do not know.

He is looking at her now. She glances away, down at the floor tiles. They are red. Nadine's false nail lies there beside her foot. A small heart.

Gustave's voice fills the image. So I will give you two options. You can leave now, while my daughter is out. Leave now and this will be the end of it. I will say no more about this situation, and nor will you. Or, if you will not leave, you must tell me what you want. Is it money?

Her glass is empty. Her eyes tremble – above his head, out of the window. She feels faint.

I could, of course, explain to Oscar that you are here in Paris. Stalking me. That would change things, wouldn't it?

A click from the front door.

Nadine is talking before she has made it down the hallway, about how their order was prepared early so the guy from the restaurant was coming up the street towards her, because they thought they might as well deliver it. She is entirely unaware of the atmosphere she has entered, slicing through it with two white carrier bags emanating sweet rich smells and dumping them on the worktop between them.

Perfect, Gustave responds, but his eyes are dead. This time when he drinks he swallows everything.

Nadine moves around them both, looking for plates in cupboards.

I found your nail, she says, picking it up from the floor.

Oh! Great. The teenager takes it from her, placing it onto the finger where it had previously been, holding it there, contemplating. Papa, does Christine have glue for this? Nadine's open grin: a life raft.

Gustave, silent now and not looking at anyone, opens a drawer directly beneath the worktop and pulls out a fistful of metal cutlery. The gesture is sharp, cutlery clanking against itself. He carries it to a dining table across the space. It is lit by a lamp hanging from a long wire above.

She reaches for the wine nearby and fills her glass. Watches Gustave's turned back. That giveaway patch of balding on his scalp. She downs her drink in one go, then refills it before picking up the bottle and taking it to the table. Anything I can do to help? she asks with a light and assured tone.

Approaching the table, she registers that the food inside the containers being laid out by Gustave and Nadine is Chinese. She had expected French food. Not greasy, artificial food. A new terrifying prospect rears its head: she must eat in front of Gustave, who is now making an obliging gesture for her to sit. Nadine is already sitting down, holding up her broken nail to the light.

She counts five seconds before submitting to Gustave's gesture. The available seat is directly opposite him. Her hand comes automatically to her fork, closing around it, but then nothing more. She has no desire to eat at all.

Nadine has spooned rice onto her own plate, passing the container to her father. You are not hungry? Nadine says.

Oh. Sorry. I was just. I mean no. I'm not very hungry. Sorry.

You're so British. Nadine takes another container and empties it onto her plate, noodles writhing. Have some noodles.

Cutlery stands in Gustave's fists, blades pointed up.

So, tell me. How did you come across Nadine?

She hopes Nadine will interrupt. But there is only the sound of chewing and the scraping of cutlery from the teenager.

I was… she starts, then stops. Nauseous. I was sitting on a bench, looking for, erm. Life models.

Gustave's upper lip curls as his teeth take on a beansprout. But what drew you to her?

Papa – Nadine, at last – I told you. She's an artist. She finds her models in the street, in public places. She saw me at the school.

The room is swimming.

Nadine turns to her. Right?

She nods, begins nudging food around her plate.

Gustave pushes a prawn into his mouth. Did you not find it strange, Nadine, that she just happened to be waiting outside the school? He gestures vaguely with his knife. Just hanging around?

Nadine looks between them with a shade of uncertainty. A signal. She's not a sex trafficker. We checked.

She sets down her fork. How else could I have found her?

Gustave masticates. There is grease at the corner of his lip. I don't know. Perhaps you came across her on social media? Facebook? He is putting on an amicably enquiring tone.

No, she responds, refilling her drink.

She's a real artist, papa. She went to the Slade.

Gustave is cutting something on his plate and asks, What is that? without looking up.

It's a very prestigious art school, she says before Nadine can answer, a buzz from the wine finally loosening her tongue. In London. It's part of University College London. You may have heard of it.

I just find it strange, he presses, that you just so happened to be in Paris and you just so happened to be outside my daughter's school and it just so happened that you are an artist and that she is the perfect model for you.

What do you find strange about that? Do you think your daughter couldn't be someone's muse?

The shades of Nadine's face shift again – she is stung by this potential judgement of her father. Gustave pretends not to notice.

For a moment nobody eats or drinks anything.

Papa. Nadine sounds younger suddenly. You know that I want to study art history? Well, we have been talking about it. She thinks it would be a good career choice for me. There are so many more options than you think… It's not just… As her father appears to ignore her, Nadine trails off, looking to her for backup. Tell him what you said to me. She is a real artist and I think you should listen to her. How different it is to studying fine art. Because, papa, this is what you do not understand—

Gustave has been laying down his cutlery with deliberate slowness. Now he brings a hand around his daughter's wrist. Do not tell me what I do not understand.

Nadine tries to pull her hand away. Her father's eyes implore her to behave. We will not have this conversation now. He releases her wrist and picks up his cutlery again as if nothing strange has taken place.

She watches the teenager stare at her plate, despondent before readjusting, going to pick up a fork.

Why not.

Father and daughter look at her. She refills her glass.

She really wants to do it, Gustave. Why can't you support her?

Nadine is nodding, mouth opening and stuttering. Yes. Papa, in a few months I will make my applications. I want to go to the Courtauld. Like I told you before.

The Courtauld. Gustave is shaking his head. Non.

Why won't you let her do what she wants with her life?

Gustave's chest heaves with a single steadying breath. He flashes his eyes at her. This does not concern you, he warns.

The next time Nadine speaks it is in French. There is a rapid back-and-forth between them. The next second Nadine is standing so fast her chair tips backwards and lands loudly, smacking against the floor tiles. Even Gustave is startled. Nadine is jabbing a finger at him. His face freezes, suggesting his daughter has said something of significance, before gesticulating in return, écoute. The teenager's voice wobbles, becomes uneven in pitch. Then she is walking quickly away, voice now fully raised, across the room. Her father stands. Nadine, he shouts. The name is a command to stop.

From the door, the teenager looks at her. Tears running down her cheeks. Come on, she is saying to her, let's go.

She stays seated. Looks at Gustave. Looks at Nadine.

Please.

Gustave looks at her as if to say: Well?

She stays seated.

The teenager is glaring now. You are both fucking assholes.

The front door slams. She flinches.

Is this what you wanted?

Why didn't you sleep with me while you had the chance?

What. Gustave's face expresses something like bemusement. Is that what this is all about? Now he is walking towards her. Instinctively she stands and backs away, circling around the table.

No. I just don't understand why, if you were just playing with me, why you didn't take it while you could?

He follows her. You want it? Now? Is that what it would take?

You started it. You were, you were staring at me, being nice to me, then you emailed me—

Oh please. I did not ask you to come here. I didn't ask you to ruin my life. I will burn that fucking drawing. He comes closer, his face shiny, repulsive. Skin red.

Her legs wobble. Trying to steady herself, she knocks over her glass of wine. It rolls over the table and shatters at his feet. The sound of glass rings against tile. He stops. She stops too.

He is breathing heavily again. I did not sleep with you – he separates out each syllable like he is English and she is not – because I... I realized what I was doing and stopped myself.

Because of your wife?

His mouth twists, sour. That's obvious, no?

She presses her fingernails into her skin. I love you.

Gustave stares at her as if he has not heard.

She says it again.

He is laughing now.

I know there is something between us, she says over his laughter. I don't mind everything that has happened. She looks down at the shattered glass, the spill of wine on the tiles like urine. You made me want you. And now you don't want me and I don't know what to do.

Gustave has stopped laughing. There it is, laid out for him. He rubs his eyes, not grinning any more. Exhales. Shakes his head. Gives a self-deprecating raise of the eyebrows. She reads his thoughts: Why does this always happen to me? She has become surmountable.

Nothing more can happen between us, he says. So I apologize for... giving any wrong impressions. But this must end here.

She sniffs, rubbing her nose then tugging down her sleeves in a way she knows makes her look childlike, vulnerable.

You understand, if Nadine ever finds out... The nature of. He flicks a hand between them. This. It will really hurt her. She thinks you are her friend.

She nods, sniffing again. What happens now?

You will leave now and go back to London. And you will

withdraw your allegations. And you will never speak to my daughter again.

Please. If I can't have you, let me have her.

What? After all this, you think I would let you run around influencing her? Absolutely not.

She pushes out her bottom lip, managing a gagged and dry sob. Then: I love Nadine.

First you love me and now you love my daughter.

I love Paris. I want to live here.

Don't be a fool.

I don't have any money to get home.

That is not my problem. You must leave now. He makes a dramatic show of checking his watch, then places two hands on a chair. His expression is set, expecting her to do as he says. Expecting this to be the end. As though this is for him to decide.

She clears her throat. I just. I'm just going to. Sort myself out. Where is your bathroom?

No, he is saying. No, please. Just leave now. I want you gone before anyone comes back.

She is already entering a corridor at the other end of the apartment. Behind her, she can sense a change in demeanour. A sudden loss of control.

You cannot stay, Gustave shouts.

Through the doorway on her left, there is a bathroom. Windowless and tiled throughout. A wet room. Antique taps. Very nice antique taps. On her right, the glimpse of a bed through the door.

No. Not in there.

She enters and closes the door behind her. To the right of the door there is an artfully distressed chair, which she picks up and tilts so that it rests under the door handle. It's something she has seen in films.

Gustave thunders up the hallway. Come out of there now, he shouts. But the power of his voice is muffled. The door handle rattles but the door remains shut. She marvels. It works. Gustave swears. Kicks. Then stops. Pressing her ear against the door, she can hear him breathe, standing there on the other side while he makes a decision. He is panicking. Eventually she hears him walk away. A pause. Then the sound of glass shards scraping along tiles. He is clearing up the mess. A laugh leaves her. Ha. Ha ha. Scary Gustave. Scary Gustave, wearing a turtleneck and serving Sauvignon Blanc with the air of someone completely in control of the situation. Ha ha ha ha ha.

She slips her foot out of her elegant flat. Her toes are red, feet blistered. She presses them into the carpet, where they are soothed and cooled by the thick pile. She takes off her other shoe. There is a super-king-size bed with a crushed velvet headboard. From the bedroom window she can see the trees of a park, a bistro with tables and chairs on the street, people sat in groups. Even from this distance she can see they are smiling, laughing. The top of someone's head as they cycle past. Sky moulting cirrus clouds. Paris busy, Paris silent.

She turns. Stops. There is another person in the room. She stands in front of a long mirror fixed to a tall wardrobe. She brings her hands up to meet those of her glass-self and slides open the door to find the clothes hanging inside. Navy, black, some pink, some white, ivory, cream. Beige. Above: racks of shoes. Heels, trainers, and there: elegant flats. In navy, black, silver, camel, grey, red. Ha ha. She slips her fingers into the folds of clothes, coming to whole suits in body bags. She breathes deeply so that the material fills her nostrils, catching the end of it – Gustave's scent.

She leaves the wardrobe open and turns to the bed. She pulls at the corner of the duvet and climbs in. The sheets are crisp and cold. There are several pillows, all crushed velvet, matching shades of beige. She flings them away. Her weight settles and the mattress shapes itself for her. Memory foam. Nice. Spreading out her arms, she imagines a body either side of her. Room for all three of them: Gustave, Christine and her. Imagines how the two of them sleep together: holding each other, or maybe curled away. How it might be to sleep between them, their wants and needs and conflicts all bleeding into her. She conjures a hologram of Gustave, climbing over her like a spider.

The door handle rattles again. Gustave tells her to come out of the room, come out now.

It is comfortable in here. Everything in neutral colours. No clutter, except for the cushions all over the carpet. On the window side of the bed, there is a small table, a bottle of perfume. She crawls across the mattress to reach it. She sprays at the base of her neck, on each of her wrists. Brings her wrist to her nose. Expensive. Then she performs a continuous spray up into the air above her head so that the particles fall onto her skin and hair, cool and revitalizing. She places the bottle back on the bedside table, next to three slim silver rings and a bracelet she picks up and spins between her fingers. Christine's slim wrist is in her hand. She holds it in the air: a viewfinder.

On the wall there is a small, framed photograph. A little girl with blonde hair, mouth red, teeth missing, arms around the shoulders of a man who has one eye closed, smiling. A younger Gustave. The girl grips the neck of a cuddly toy. A goose.

I will call the police, Gustave is shouting. Or I break this door down. He rattles the handle again.

She knows he will not break down the door. And to call the police would require an explanation of things. Embarrassing for him. She gets out of the bed, considering whether to collect up the cushions and remake it. No. He can deal with that. She then considers whether to bleed on the bed. No, that would be more abject than eating in front of him.

Gustave has stopped shouting. She listens at the door. He is talking in the kitchen. It is difficult to make out his words. Perhaps he really is calling the police. She removes the chair from the door and opens it, preparing to bolt through the living room when she registers that there are not one but two people out there, a woman in a long green coat with her back to her. She freezes. Starts to take a step back. But it is too late.

Oh. Hello. Christine is giving a polite smile. English accent.

She looks at Gustave. He looks away. The table has been cleared, chairs replaced, no glass on the floor.

Christine falters. Her eyes are blue and sad. Sorry. Are you…

I'm the. She stops, swallowing. I'm the artist. I mean. Nadine's friend? You might—

Sorry. For some mad reason I thought you had just broken in. Christine presses the back of her hand against her forehead, showing slim wrists. Nadine's told me a lot about you. Her accent: southern English, home counties. Middle class.

She feels exposed, her bones stripped bare, as Christine's gaze runs down her before she turns to Gustave.

Where's Nadine?

She has, uh, gone out. She was upset.

Again?

He nods once and Christine lays a comforting hand on his forearm.

She watches them, husband and wife closing off to her now.

What about you? she asks loudly. Who are you?

It has the desired effect. Christine is back, surprised. Me? Oh, sorry. I'm Christine.

Christine. Saying the name out loud for the first time. Something is birthed from her mouth, a connection. Joining the end of a line to make a circle. The things she has been chasing, the things that form this life – the people, the attachments – here in the room with her now. She has done it. This life is hers to break apart. To destruct and therefore own.

Having not said anything else for a long time, she is staring at Christine, who is starting to look disconcerted.

Okay, Gustave says. Let's not keep you. You've got a flight to catch, non?

She ignores him, her attention on Christine. Where in England are you from?

Cambridge.

Right. So you were just. She spreads her hands. Born into this life.

Christine is pretending to understand, smiling politely again.

She is beautiful. She might once have been a model. A model at her own age now. To break this couple apart would mean nothing, Christine would simply glide away. Or worse, she would have the grace to forgive Gustave. She is nice because her world is nice. Even worse, they would make it work because Gustave and Christine actually love each other. How must that feel? In the face of this, she is a speck.

How did you two meet?

Gustave adjusts his weight from one foot to another. Makes a pained sound under his breath, directed at Christine. A plea.

Through friends, Christine answers.

Through friends. Of course neither of them use Tinder. Gustave and Christine meeting through friends – all of them wearing turtlenecks. Gustave and Christine spotting one another across the room. Who approached who? Or perhaps they were drawn together. Just a natural conversation, a spark. They just found themselves together. What could they possibly have in common, except that they are from the same world.

The world she herself has no access to, no passage except via another.

Sorry, Christine is saying. I'm staring because you look familiar. We haven't met before, have we?

Gustave's brow deepens, eyes widening with new concern.

We live in completely different worlds, she replies. Actually, I need to go. Gustave – she pronounces it how he taught her in the hotel room – was just buying my ticket back to London. A gift. For the. For the drawing of Nadine.

Gustave appears to go through something internally, then composes himself. Yes. You leave tonight, he says.

Tomorrow.

He hesitates. Then concedes: Tomorrow.

Oh, hang on. Christine has approached her quickly, wrapping her fingers around her arm. Such soft, cool hands. I know what it is now. Christine turns back to Gustave, who looks more panicked than ever. Doesn't she look like your mother? No? Well I think it's remarkable. Were you originally French?

The time is 05:32 when Gustave sends her a plane ticket, the flight leaving in four hours.

I can't get to the airport, she writes immediately.

I will book you an Uber, he replies.

Her thumbs are angled, preparing to write again. What to write. She wants to hold on to him. Keep him in her life somehow. Then his profile photo disappears, the circle it once filled becoming grey. His status disappears. He has blocked her.

In the lift, she closes her eyes. When the sudden jolt of gravity passes through her body she cannot tell if she is going up or down. She wants to be going up.

The doors part for the final time. The final time for her, at least. Other people will come to Paris, will come to this hotel, stay in her room. She pauses, but there is someone outside the lift waiting to use it.

The immaculate female receptionist asks if she enjoyed her stay.

Yes, thank you, she responds. I don't ever want to leave.

The receptionist smiles, reading her as just another gushing tourist and not someone whose life right now depends on staying.

She taps her key card on the desk. Clearing her throat, she asks, Do you know if there's, like, anywhere for people to stay when they have no money. Just, you know. If someone did want to stay here, but they had no money.

You mean… here? The receptionist points downwards.

No, not in this hotel. Just in Paris.

The receptionist's eyes flick to her computer briefly, then

back to her, and with a gentle shake of her head and a gentle ripple of her ponytail, she says, No. Sorry.

She is still tapping her key card on the desk, an irritating sound. Do you know anyone who might want to buy a plane ticket to London?

Now the receptionist is frowning at her. What?

She lets the key card clatter onto the desk. Forget it.

On the street, she puts a cigarette in her mouth, then takes it out and throws it away. She finds a cafe opening, with white fluorescent lighting. Pastries in the windows. She takes a window seat, gets out her phone and downloads Tinder. She looks for photos to upload. The first is a selfie from the hotel room, taken because her hair looked good, her skin looked good. Something about the way the light fell through the windows, reflecting across the white interior, reflecting onto her. The next photo is of the sculpture. The next: herself again, in her flat in Southend, making coffee with a cigarette in her mouth.

A woman wearing white overalls shouts from behind the counter, intonation suggesting that she is being asked what she wants.

Oh. A coff… nothing. Nothing, thanks.

Pardon?

Nothing, I'm good. Thanks.

On her phone she swipes right right right right right right. No matches.

Glancing over her shoulder, she finds that the woman behind the counter is staring at her.

She points down at her seat. Can I sit here for a bit?

No.

But I don't have any money, she says.

The woman looks angry.

She looks at her phone once more, then picks up her bag, bringing it to her shoulder with one hand, still swiping. Right right right right right right.

A match!

It is raining. She stands under an awning on the corner of the street and messages her Tinder match. Bastien, 29. Dirty blonde hair. Wearing a brown jacket and reading a book. Perfect.

Bonjour. I'm an English girl in Paris.

She waits for Bastien's reply. After three minutes, she writes another message: *Could you show me around?* Casual, not desperate. A projection in the near future: maybe fifteen minutes, thirty minutes, maybe an hour, a couple of hours, she will arrive at Bastien's apartment, hair artfully damp, spontaneous and interesting. The rain falls harder. She considers writing another message. The pavements are empty. Passing cars spray water over the kerb. She needs another profile in the local area. But her screen is blank. No connection. She refreshes. Swipes right, swipes left. Down. Up. A text message – your mobile data. To purchase add-ons, call…

She wanders Paris. At one point a man follows her, at times walking backwards alongside her, looking into her face, trying out words, phrases in French and then English, asking why isn't she talking, where is she from, where is she going, is she scared, why is she scared. She crosses the road to get away from him, but as she does so he grabs at her and the sensation of his hands on her body goes through her, a shock. She pulls away, tripping as she does. Begins to run. Her phone rings, a number with a French dialling code. Gustave?

Hello?

A man is speaking French at the other end. She glances over her shoulder. The other man is hanging back but still following.

Uber, the caller says. Uber. À l'hôtel.

.

SOUTHEND

She grips the handrail at the top of the plane steps, unable to move. The people waiting behind her start to tut. Other passengers on the tarmac below shield their eyes, looking up at the novelty of a person who will not leave the plane. The stairs are too high. Too steep. The sun is too bright. Everything is aflame. The ground. The runway. She tries to back up, return to her seat, but the air steward is there, face concerned but firm, directing her towards the stairs again.

In the Arrivals passageway, she stops and sits down on the floor while other passengers from other planes pass by. Two people in hi-vis vests approach and ask her if she is okay.

She says, Yes.

Are you unwell?

Do I look unwell.

One of them looks at the other one but pretends not to. We must ask you to move along, please, they say.

She looks away.

You can't stay here. You can sit down once you've gone through passport control.

I just don't want to go home yet.

At passport control the self-service machine shows a sallow and angry image of herself, then rejects her. She tries again, and again. She is told to queue to see an actual person. This person compares her with her passport. She is waved through.

Arrivals is full of people leaving the airport, of crowds thinning out. All signs to exits, taxis, buses, car parks, trains… from where she will have to get another train. Because there is now nowhere else to go. I hate it here, she thinks.

I hate it here.

I hate it here.

A slipping stack of envelopes on the laminate floor. Her flat feels smaller than she remembers, growing smaller and moving away from her. She sits on the bed and opens Instagram. An image under *#frenchgirlstyle*: a girl who wears a vintage jacket and walks down a street in Paris, hair cut short but so feminine, so beautiful and so easy, so undeniably French.

In the bathroom she twists a strip of hair between her fingers, going cross-eyed in order to angle the scissors up close and cut. She repeats with another strip, her phone propped up behind the taps, the image of the girl at a slight angle. She approximates the basic shape of it, where the fringe and sides fall, calculating roughly how the back might look. Snip. Snip. She cuts up from the collarbone, grazing her shoulders. She cuts and cuts and expects the look to be complete at some point, but it is not quite right. She looks like a boy. In the sink the hair has formed a seabed.

She slumps down against the wall. She brings the washing machine door to her face. The glass is cool on her forehead, her flat warped beyond.

She lies on her bed with a headache. The shape of a want forming. But it is transparent, unknowable. She has her phone in one hand, empty hand curled beside for comparison. She sits up. Downloads Bumble. Downloads Hinge. Downloads Tinder. She watches the circles complete on the display screen. Stops when each app asks her to *Tell us about yourself!*

What is there to tell?

She deletes each one, then opens WhatsApp and selects Nadine. Types out: *Hey, how are you?*

Early morning. Southend High Street is empty except for seagulls picking at damp cardboard outside McDonald's. She is walking close to one side of the pedestrianized street, aware that her head is down and wanting to keep it that way. A woman sitting up in a sleeping bag, in the doorway of a bank, asks if she has any change.

She passes the cafe which only takes cash. The smell of coffee floating out of the doors sets off a craving for an oat milk flat white, an almond milk cortado, poached egg and avocado on toast with Buck's Fizz. A girl is sitting in the window, reading a book. About nineteen, twenty years old. Her trousers are nice. She must think she's the most interesting person here. That is why she is sitting in the window. She remembers how this felt: to be on the cusp of the rest of your life. She wishes she was her.

Excuse me. An elderly couple are sitting outside with a dog at their feet. One of them is talking to her. Can I just say that you've got a lovely haircut.

She takes them in, their matching coats and oldness. The hairy dog lying on the pavement. Why would you choose to grow old and die here. She walks away, knowing she should say something but not wanting to, pretending she does not speak English.

On a bench at the top of Pier Hill, water stretches below, across to Canvey Island and Kent. There is no escape. A rat passes her foot, then returns with another rat. If she closes her eyes she could pretend she is another person in another place. There is a downward slope of grass and trees ending at a road before the land meets the sea. How freeing it would be to float out to sea, where the wind turbines are. Then further still: to be on her way somewhere else. To be on her way and not yet there. Could she roll down the hill and make it to the sea, or would she be hit by a car? And if she did make it? Then what? Would the tide take her out? Take her somewhere else? When she squints, the horizon disappears.

She starts walking again.

At Southend Central station, people are heading for the train. She follows them into the ticket hall. At least these people are going somewhere. A pang of nostalgia. For her former self. Her window seat.

The departures board shows the time in hours and seconds. She counts the trains to Fenchurch Street. Contemplates rushing in behind someone, through the barriers, onto the train, precisely the one arriving in one minute and twenty seconds. Running fast. Running to her spot. Prising her way through with her elbows. Finding her seat. Settling in. Her body adjusting to the seat's shape. The memory of the seat. So like an embrace. And the sensation of being on her way to somewhere else, leaving this place.

She imagines walking to Datata from Fenchurch Street. Walking up the stairs to the desks on the first floor, where the phones are ringing and a satisfied sun warms all of the faces. Oscar looking up. Jerry looking up. Green Trousers, Marketing. Everyone seeing her. From these stares, she sees herself as they see her: pale, exhausted, horrible haircut.

The drawing of Gustave is not as poor as she remembers. The sections of his face she has managed to capture are somehow more real for leading to nothing. Wide nose. A manic eye. Teeth revealing themselves. She tears it down the middle.

Sitting on the floor in front of the mirror, she tries to draw her own face.. Between her reflection and the page, something is lost. Awkward and ugly. Lines too thick. She bites the end of the pencil, leaving tooth marks – a warning. She tries again, pushing through this time, letting whatever falls out of her hand be the image. Letting it be what it is. Pencil moving quickly, finding a fluidity. Trusting her hand to find her face.

When she looks properly, what is on the page is all loose lines and circles. A pretender's drawing, someone pretending to have talent. This is my face, she thinks.

She bites the pencil again, harder. Finds the brittle centre of the lead within, and then the tooth pain returns. She screams, drawing the pencil out of her mouth and driving it down into the hand resting on the page. This secondary pain is more comforting than the throbbing one in her gums. She brings the pencil away, finding a red-black point etched into her skin.

Having fallen asleep at some point, she wakes up on the floor, drawings around her. The light outside is uncertain: it could be dawn, it could be dusk. Fingers seek out her phone on the floor.

1 missed call from Nadine.

Foreign dial tone, a single note starting and stopping, lonely and plain. Then there is a click and inside her there is a pulling downwards, like the sensation of missing a step and falling.

Hey, Nadine says.

Hi, she says automatically, quickly. Wanting to hold on to it. Nadine. Hi. Sorry, Nadine. Sorry. I've been trying to.

Nadine sighs.

Are you okay?

I had another fight with my dad. A defeated note to her voice. The Americanism: *a fight*, a more violent choice of word than merely *an argument*. An image of father and daughter, back in that open-plan apartment, throwing crockery at one another, screaming, throwing fists. The mad, angry spew of French.

What happened? Are you okay?

I'm fine.

Are you hurt?

Hurt? Why would I be. I'm fine. A pause. But basically papa said if I want to study art history then I have to do it all by myself. Pay for it myself. Pay the tuition fees, pay to live. Nadine's voice wobbles once. That's it. His final decision.

You can do it.

Nadine's anger crests and breaks through the surface. How do you know? You couldn't do it. And then you just left. You just disappeared without saying goodbye. And now I'm just stuck here and I'm not talking to my dad and I don't know what to do. No one gets it. Even my friend, she was like, it makes sense to do what your dad says because of the security. And *mama*, obviously she said that too. What does she know.

Come here.

Everyone's always against what I want.

Nadine, come here. Come and stay with me.

Another pause. Really.

Why not. We can visit all the galleries. You can model for me again. I'll paint you this time. I could make a really big painting of you. Or whatever you like. It's up to you.

I *would* like that, the teenager responds.

So come.

She hears the air leaving Nadine's nose. Maybe. I will think about it.

Okay. Well, I miss you.

Bye, Nadine replies, and the call ends.

Another phone notification, this time from her bank. PAYMENT FROM DATATA HOLDINGS LTD. Her pay cheque.

With the money she books an emergency dentist appointment. The reception is solid wood from wall to ceiling, the fluorescent lights turning it a sickly brown. The pain in her back tooth has not subsided for over twelve hours. Her hand is on her jaw, which is swollen and hot. She regards the row of blue plastic chairs, the holes in them like inverted Braille, and sits down next to another person. Immediately feeling sick. She goes to stand again, in order to walk back outside where it is dark and cold, but her blood travels in the other direction, leaving her brain, to her feet. She is unconscious before her head meets the floor.

There is a glass of water on the small table attached to the dentist's chair. Her body is burning on the inside, the heat coming out as cold sweat. The dental nurse is standing with his back to her, at a worktop, writing notes.

So there's no chance that you could be pregnant?

No. Well. Not that there's, like, no chance. I'm just not.

What do you mean? Are you sexually active? Are you using protection?

I'm not, she says again.

How are you feeling now?

Better.

The nurse glances at her over his shoulder – a medically informed look.

Her limbs are pleasantly heavy. Fainting feels like rebirth. Her head is empty. She only remembers being given water, the concern, the offer of a cup of tea. Being helped into this room, with its warm lighting and fleshy beige walls, a large jar of sugar-free lollipops on the counter. At some point the possession of a cardboard bowl was entrusted to her. It sits on her lap, dry.

I don't feel sick, she says.

Okay, the nurse replies, checking his watch.

After around fifteen minutes, a male dentist enters the room and introduces himself to her kindly. His hands are in blue latex gloves. He inspects her mouth, movements gentle, sure, firm. He explains the procedure. She nods and sniffs, looking away, tears in her eyes. Without saying anything, he turns on his swivel chair to hand her a box of tissues. It's been quite the day for you, hasn't it, he says.

She nods again, pressing a tissue to her eyes.

His surgical mask twitches to suggest he is smiling. Don't worry, he says, let's get you sorted. And she imagines the sensation of his glove – soft, powdered – patting her knee. The dental nurse is at her side now. Both men focus on her and her alone. They murmur things to one another. The dentist pushes metal utensils against her teeth. Her fingers curl over the chair arms and grip. She knows how they look together, the three of them, because she has watched root canal procedures on YouTube, multiple times. Close up: throbbing tongue, red and pink gums, rotting teeth. Between them, though, she is in her body. Her skin alive with attention. The needle enters her gum and slowly that side of her mouth goes numb. The drill is uncomfortable, and when she whimpers the dentist says soothing things. Nearly there now. Almost done. You're doing really well.

The procedure finishes. While hoovering shavings from the cavern of her face, the dentist tells her that it might still be sore for a few days, so to take paracetamol in that case. Try not to eat anything hard. If the pain continues, come back. She leans round and spits purple fluid into the sink.

The nurse asks if she smokes. She says no, catching the eye of the dentist, who is back on his stool, arms resting on his knees. His mask is still on but she knows he is smiling by the wrinkles around his eyes. When you're ready, you're free to go, he says. But please, take your time.

She does not want to go. Poking her tongue into the back of her mouth compulsively, she finds that the hole is gone, replaced by a new and rough plane. At the sensation, she realizes this compulsion, this habit, will now come to an end.

Night arrived while she was inside. She presses a lollipop to the numb side of her mouth. The flavour leaks into her saliva – lemon. There is a back alley that runs alongside a stagnant canal. Under dim lights she picks out packaging, detritus, coloured plastic vibrant under lamp-post light. Over the canal wall, she sees terraced houses, hears the theme tune to *EastEnders*. Bin bags, torn open, contents strewn across the concrete. She steps around dog shit. The canal does not end but disappears beneath the ground. The lemon flavour has started to remind her of vomit. She flicks the lollipop from her mouth and into the canal.

Back on the main road, she presses the button at a pedestrian crossing. WAIT lights up. There are no cars, but nonetheless she stands and waits. I am lost, she thinks. Surely a dental clinic cannot be the only place to feel love.

A Farrow & Ball green door opens and Jenny appears, wearing a football shirt and a smile, which changes upon registering who has knocked. Oh, your hair.

I'm not well, she says. Tears gather again.

Jenny's face glitches briefly before she says, without breath, Is it cancer?

They go up the stairs to Jenny's spare room, or what Jenny calls the *studio*, which is still a spare room because there is a bed. Around their heads, little people walk the walls, along shelves, across the top of a wardrobe. Except they are not walking, but their limbs and clothing are moulded from clay in such a way that it suggests movement. Nondescript clothing in non-specific colours with no faces, turning into the alcoves and away again, towards the window, and along the other side. They all face the same direction, affected by a phantom breeze. It is obvious that Jenny's skills have developed: finer details.

She sits on the bed. Jenny has left the room, saying she will be back in a minute. Her face must be swollen and pink but there is nothing she can do about it. She hears a low whine from somewhere, and realizes it is from her.

Sorry, she says, when Jenny returns and hands her a wad of tissue paper. I just can't stop crying.

What are you apologizing for? I'm the one that should be sorry, giving you a load of toilet roll. Jenny sits next to her and the mattress compresses and creaks. We're just about to get rid of this bed, actually. Well, once Gareth finally puts it on Freebay.

I'm not well, she says again. Then regrets it. She feels like all this might seem a little melodramatic. Showing up at Jenny's house. She gestures to the side of her face where the swelling feels more visible than it is. It's. It's this. I had root canal surgery.

Oh wow, really? Does it hurt?

Not yet.

Jenny brings up her fingers against the swelling, testing it. The closeness is uncomfortable, not what she wants. She glances away, scans the room. On a desk in the corner, something is in the midst of taking shape, surrounded by wooden sticks and plaster dust. Behind it are photos pinned to the wall. Photos of a man at different angles. A scrap of paper with numbers and measurements. Jenny is in the middle of making something.

Then the door opens and they both turn to see Jenny's boyfriend standing in the doorway, wearing a matching football shirt. Oh. You, he says. Then: Half-time is almost over, babe.

Well, I'll be down in a minute.

The boyfriend retreats. There is something about the way Jenny snapped at him that is reassuring. Sending the man away so it is just them.

God, it's only a friendly, Jenny tuts, directing this at the sculptures.

It is not just them now. It is her, Jenny, and Jenny's *art practice*.

She puts down the tissue and gets up, preparing to move towards the door and leave.

No, no. Jenny's hand holds down her arm.

She sits again.

So, is there anything else wrong?

She shrugs, staring at her knees.

I've been worried about you, Jenny says. You were behaving very weirdly at the pub and then… well, you know what happened. Then not a word since.

You haven't contacted me either.

It can't always be me reaching out to you. And it seemed like you needed some space. But now you've shown up here, crying. So why don't we try to sort it out.

She pretends to check her fingernails, thumb picking at skin. What is there to *sort out*.

What do you think? The pub, this. What was going on with Waheed? I told you he was engaged and you were all over him.

She tucks away her fingers. Actually, *he* was all over me.

Jenny stares back at her, then stands, blocking out the sculpture on the desk. Don't you have any self-respect?

She rolls her eyes performatively.

You just. You just have this thing about men. Jenny is flapping her hands. It's a problem. Just shagging random men all the time. Look. I'm sex positive, aren't I. I'm not trying to shame you—

You obviously are.

Well. There's a limit, isn't there? Jenny stops, rubbing her lips together, preparing words which have likely been rehearsed at some point, spun around Jenny's mind, biting nails in front of the television as she asked her boyfriend, over and over, what she should do, what she should say to the problem friend. I think you need help, she finishes.

Ha. She rubs her nose with the back of her hand. Okay. What kind of *help* do I need.

Jenny shrugs loosely. I don't know. But you're so bloody despondent all the time. Are you depressed?

She stares.

You see where I'm coming from, though? You've turned up all hysterical with your hair hacked off—

It's none of your business, actually.

Jenny's arms flap once more and she consults the room in exasperation. I don't get it. I don't get why you've come here and now you won't open up to me. You've never really opened up to me… It's like we aren't even friends any more.

I didn't realize there were *criteria* to being *friends*. Why even bother staying in touch with me.

That's what I'm asking now, Jenny says.

She glares, tightening her arms around herself. You know. You have all these *principles*, you say all these things. But you just make the same thing over and over again—

What? Sorry – what has this got to do with anything?

We can't all just live off art. We haven't all got boyfriends who work in property development who can pay—

193

Oh my god. Not this again.

I just want something more from life than making things for people to *buy*.

Jenny makes a noise of disbelief. Like what? Are you just going to keep working shitty temping jobs until you die?

She shakes her head. I bet you didn't want me to know that you'd gone out without me that night.

Jenny's posture changes, chin lifting. I go out without you all the time. You're not my only mate. We were out celebrating. And you ruined it.

Her gaze ticks across the room to where Jenny's hands rest at her middle, realizing she has been fiddling there for some time and has now stopped: among the chunky vintage rings on her hand, there is a new one. Gold with a neat diamond. She pretends not to have seen it, wanting Jenny to have to say it. But something compels her. I bet *he* proposed to *you*, didn't he.

Yeah. Jenny's voice is even now. Yeah, he did.

It wasn't some. Some kind of *conversation*, then. Some decision made together as an equal partnership. And a diamond. How *feminist* of you.

Christ, it's like everything is a chance for you to make out that you're better than me. What do you think this is about? Not all relationships are just transactions.

Her mouth opens and then closes, the insinuation of Jenny's remark landing before she can get out what she had prepared to say. She decides not to look at Jenny. Decides instead to look at the skirting board, an area of newly applied white gloss paint, achieved in two streaks, one short and one long. She spots a short hair stuck beneath the surface. How could Jenny allow that.

I love him, Jenny is saying, and I want to be with him for the rest of my life.

Well, if that's what you want. She gets up and moves past Jenny, who takes a step back. She goes to the desk and picks up the work in progress. It is cold to the touch and heavy, an uncanny weight to it. As she lifts it, she turns to see Jenny next to her, crowned by the sculptures above her head, with an expression she has never seen before.

Could you put that down, Jenny is saying. That's a commission. It's not finished yet.

It is cold because it is still wet. There are the beginnings of a brow, the shape of the eyes, the nose. It already looks just like the photographs. She presses her thumb against it. Just malleable enough for the detailing to be smudged away.

Jenny has moved forward, saying, Mate, please—

She bats off Jenny's reaching hand and holds the maquette aloft. Jenny freezes, hands out, wanting to rescue her work, but she knows, and she knows that Jenny knows, that to prise it from her fingers would cause further damage. Don't call me mate, she says. We're not even friends, remember?

Could you put it down. You're freaking me out.

How much are you getting for it.

Nine hundred, if you must know.

Nine hundred?

Yes. Nine hundred. Now could you—

She jerks her wrist rapidly as though to throw it. This has the desired effect: Jenny reaches out to catch it, but her hands remain empty.

Nine hundred is not a lot for a custom piece like this, is it? Considering how much work you're putting into it.

Okay, okay, fine. It's one thousand five hundred. Okay? Rounded up.

Jenny's confession then apparent embarrassment about the price has a double-edged flavour to it: sweet, then bitter. Jenny is close enough for her to see the mascara smudged beneath her waterline, and two spots emerging, red beneath concealer.

Who is it?

Someone's dad. Someone asked me to make their dad. For his sixtieth birthday. Look, I need to have it finished by—

She lets the sculpture go. It thumps against Jenny's palms as she catches it, but the force of it is obviously a shock, and Jenny's grasp slips and the sculpture rolls out of her fingers, onto the floor, where it thumps again. Oh my god, shit, Jenny is saying, crouching down to retrieve it.

Leaving Jenny in the room, she walks out onto the landing, down the stairs, nearing the front door. She passes the living room and sees Jenny's boyfriend, broad back and shoulders hunched, watching football on the television. Jenny's *fiancé*.

He turns, saying, Everything okay, babe? But on seeing her, his face hardens. Oh. It's you, he says.

The tide is in and the sea is black. She stands on a small strip of shingle, where the water threatens to touch her. The Thames Estuary water. She imagines filling her mouth with it. Infecting her tooth, her gums and then returning to the dentist for him to lay her down and tend to her again, treating her gently and softly and reassuringly. Maybe he liked her. What was his name? Perhaps she can google him.

On her phone, the image of Nadine vibrates. She answers.

I'm coming tomorrow, Nadine says. I just booked the Eurostar with my dad's credit card.

Along the horizon a giant cargo ship, near invisible in the dark, passes. A shadow in transit.

Have you told him you're coming here?

No. Will you paint me?

Yes. Yes, I'll paint you.

Okay. See you soon. I can't wait.

When she walks along the beach, the shingle breaks over her Converse sneakers, *the laid-back staple for any Parisian's off-duty wardrobe.*

In the morning she buys a large canvas almost twice her height and four times her armspan. She buys primer, new brushes, paint. She grazes her knuckles on the walls as she takes everything up the stairs to her flat.

At 15:00 she meets Nadine off the Eurostar. When Nadine embraces her, she is overcome again by that thing, that thing previously beyond reach, a sensation she might describe as feeling whole, or full. Nadine determinedly warm in an oversized Nike hoodie, the slant of her walk, slouch of her shoulders, the ease of wealth trickling down from her father, Nadine wrapping long arms around her, clean and good-smelling, loved and loving. It spreads across to her own body and enters it. Yes: it is fullness.

Nadine does not say anything about her hair, apparently not noticing. But she talks. Talks and talks. She wants to see all of London now, go to the Tate Modern, go to a pub, go to a club. She doesn't understand why they are leaving the city, where Southend is. She says she was thinking of getting a hotel, or some Airbnb. Scenery outside turns from grey to green, yellow, and then the sea.

All my materials are at my flat, is all she says. And besides, if you use your dad's credit card, he'll know where you're staying.

Right. Nadine chews her sleeve, then says, But don't you live in London?

I basically live in London.

—

Leaving Southend Central station, the world becomes smaller, Nadine bigger. The sky draws in, tightening. A car with customized bumpers and boosted bass passes. The ground vibrates. Nadine's presence seems to ricochet off the environment, making everything louder, uglier. Seagulls call in the sky, spiralling, as though circling a new force. Unlike her, Nadine is not contained by this place.

See? The train only took, what, an hour and a half? She feels pathetic saying this. Nadine does not respond, preoccupied by the scenes inside Wetherspoons as they pass, staring until her suitcase is upturned by something caught on the wheel.

It takes ten minutes to reach the top of her road now. She experiences a deep dread. Bringing Nadine here has made things worse. Living here means Nadine will know: she is this place.

Do you want to get a coffee or something? Instead of going to mine.

Nadine's head flops back. I am so tired.

Right, but—

Nadine stops on the pavement, groaning. And we've been walking foreverrrrrrr.

She contemplates the teenager in protest. She could run and the teenager would be lost here forever.

Turning, she heads back in the direction of the flat. Listens for the sound of the suitcase rolling after her, which it eventually does. The entrance hallway smells of smoke. How had she not noticed it before. How had she not noticed how filthy it is. Promotional leaflets scattered. Black mould. They walk up the stairs, suitcase clunking behind. She wishes they could be any other two people.

Nadine follows her into her flat. She watches the teenager's back as she takes in the bed, the fridge and hob and microwave, all in one room. The MDF wardrobe. Light without a lamp-shade. A single-glazed window. Cobwebs. Not-white walls.

Where will I sleep?

The bed.

And where will you sleep?

The bed.

Nadine's head stops on seeing the large canvas propped against the radiator. She gazes at it for a few seconds. Speaks at last to say, I need to use the bathroom.

She waits for Nadine to close the door behind her, then steps up onto her bed, reaching up and tearing down the dangling cobweb with her hand. It sticks to her. She rubs it roughly against her thigh, where it bundles together. Then she scrapes it off her palm, watching it fall to the floor, where she kicks it under the bed.

Nadine opens the bathroom door and is still like a giant, surveying the room again, moving towards the window and singing *Neewwwww Yoooorrrrrk, concrete jungle where dreams are made of.*

She knows that all that Nadine can see is the rough patch of land with nothing on it except an empty skip. She fills the kettle. The sound of it crackling and screeching into action is loud enough to suspend any further exchange. She takes out the *nice cups* from the cupboard, two mugs she bought from Anthropologie the day she signed the rental agreement on this flat, thinking these would be good for company whenever she had a friend round to chat. Or something.

The kettle clicks and becomes silent. Steam gathers and re-mains. There is condensation on the window.

Do you want coffee?

For a moment Nadine does not answer, eyes shifting around the floor. I'm kind of hungry, actually, she says, moving around her, jumper-hands closing around cupboard handles, opening and shutting. Wow, you have, like, nothing.

They go to the seaside, and Nadine takes on a different energy. The sun emerges. Long grass and yellow flowers are bright along the cinder path towards the fishing village. Sitting on a wall, they are the same height.

Nadine asks what this is.

A cockle, she replies. You put vinegar on it. And pepper.

Nadine does so, piercing it on a plastic fork and putting it in her mouth. Chewing, then wordlessly going for another one. Gulls call, as though having followed them. With the fork Nadine gestures to the land on the other side of the sea, with its industrial buildings, and asks what place that is.

France, she says.

Nadine holds the polystyrene tray out to her. The cold shell-fish glistens. Gross. Her stomach is too tight. She gestures it away. Nadine continues eating.

I think I'm going to try and be an artist, she says.

But you already are one, Nadine says flatly.

I mean, to actually do it. Sell my artwork.

Nadine chews, looking thoughtful. Okay.

I thought you'd be pleased.

Sure. But you said it would be, like, impossible. And you should be doing it for you. Not to please me.

An acute pain in her palm. She lifts her hand to see a small white piece of shingle lodged in. I'm not doing it to please you. She flicks the shingle away and it tumbles over the wall, hitting the sand below without sound. It leaves an indented shape in her palm.

Can we go to London tomorrow, Nadine is saying now.

We're already in London.

The teenager gives her a look which she pretends not to see.

She gestures at the water. How can this not be London. This is the Thames.

Nadine sets down the polystyrene tray and claps her hands together twice, removing imaginary dirt. I believe it, she responds. The water looks like shit.

She laughs.

Then Nadine explains she's signed herself up to an open day at the Courtauld tomorrow. That is why they *must* go to London.

Top to tail in her bed. The night is cast blue through her thin curtains. She looks down her nose at Nadine's form against the headboard, knowing how charcoal would capture her face in the dark. No – blue pastel. No – the square press of a brush. Is she looking at her? Is she asleep? The shadows render her eyeless. Then the mattress begins to shift, an uneasy sea. Nadine is diving under the duvet, emerging again, face beside her. Nadine sets down her pillow alongside hers and spreads an arm over her loosely, hand resting on her stomach, her head resting a breath away from hers. She wills herself not to feel the vitality of the arm, of Nadine around her, but it is pinning her down onto the bed. This is the same as falling off the edge of the world. She holds herself still, corpse-like, unaware of time passing until the teenager's breath changes, the warm and the cool against her ear.

In the morning she wakes to find Nadine turned away from her. She moves around, stretching, yawning, coughing to wake her up, but Nadine stays asleep. Finally she presses her finger to the teenager's shoulder blade. Nadine turns slowly, squinting. She stares at her for a few seconds, as if she's confused, disorientated. Then Nadine brushes her arm over her face and says, For a moment I thought you were my friend. And laughs.

Aren't I?

Yawning behind rubbing hands, Nadine says, No, no. I mean my friend. Chloe.

She stands in the kitchenette, drinking coffee and thinking about her haircut. The teenager's suitcase is open on the floor and the insides have been pulled out, making a trail of clothes to the bathroom, where Nadine is having a shower. EDM can be heard behind the wall and beneath the water. She crouches down and picks through the teenager's belongings. Sweatshirts, jeans. Sports socks. Two pairs of trainers. Floral underwear – oddly girlish. A small gold necklace, tangled. Hearing the shower stop and door open, she drops the necklace and stands. Nadine emerges, wrapped in a towel. Face rubbed, eyes wider and darker, hair wet and slicked back.

Do you have a. Oh.

Nadine moves towards the hairdryer plugged in on the floor. Pads wet feet through her clothes. *French women embrace the natural texture of their hair. So put down that hairdryer! Get rid of those straighteners! Just let it air-dry, baby.* The hairdryer is on and Nadine is tipping her head upside down. The smell of hair products heating fills the room. She watches the teenager dry her hair loosely, opening the wardrobe with her free hand and flicking through what is there. There is a slight downward tip of her chin when she pulls out something – a shirt – to observe it.

Hey. Can I wear this?

Yes, she says too quickly.

Nadine chucks it onto the bed and pushes her arm into the wardrobe again. The hairdryer drones on briefly then stops. Oh no, Nadine is saying, pulling out an unremarkable top. I want to wear this.

You can wear what you want, she says. Meaning it.

You have a lot of black, Nadine replies. Flicking on the hairdryer once more, she pulls out other things and casts them on the bed. With one item she stops mid-throw, scrunches her nose and returns it to the wardrobe. Then, hair dried and flicked frizzy at the ends, Nadine starts to get dressed with a face of deep concentration.

She looks down at her coffee. There are particles in the surface, possibly a thin film of hair product. Can I wear something of yours?

Sure.

All the clothes look so plain, really: all oversized and branded. In Nadine's too-big hoodie she looks about twelve years old. Should I do something with my hair?

The teenager looks at her – really looks at her – and she feels herself shrinking on the inside. The feeling is worse when Nadine runs her fingers through her hair, scraping it into some kind of shape. There. It looks fine now. Nadine pulls on a pair of her trousers, which are transformed. Do you think I look like a curator? the teenager gasps to herself in the mirror, adjusting the shirt hem. Or even an *art historian*?

Over Nadine's shoulder she tries to see any discernible

change in her hair. I have been doing things wrong all the time, she thinks.

They wait for the train at Southend Central. Nadine asks her why she lied about living in London. I didn't, she replies.

Nadine scoffs. You think I'm stupid.

She checks the time. People from here always say it. Especially if they're from Essex. It's just easier. London is near. And everyone knows London. No one knows Essex.

I have heard of Essex, Nadine says.

Well then. Another reason why we say we're from London.

The train pulls in.

Nadine sits in an empty six-seater at the window, facing forward. She sits opposite. The past disappears before her, although the simulation is wrong, with Nadine sitting where her past is supposed to be. Nadine's eyes jump back and forth to take in the passing scenery. She presses a fingertip to the glass, saying, Oh look, that's where we were yesterday.

Someone boards the train and sits next to them.

Nadine grabs her phone from her pocket. Flashes her the screen to show it is ringing. It's papa, she says.

Block him.

I can't block him.

She leans in. Their knees are touching. Look at me. She waits until the teenager reluctantly looks back at her. Block him.

The upside-down view of Nadine's phone. The small circular photo of Gustave in sunglasses disappearing. Nadine pulls a mock grimace, then presses the buttons until he is *Blocked*. Then pushes away her phone again. They both grin.

In the courtyard of the Courtauld, water from fountains stabs at the air and fails, slapping back onto the concrete over and over.

A group of young people gather at the entrance, behind red banners and rope. The queue is greeted by two people wearing blazers, smiling and holding clipboards. Nadine is moving towards it all, long legs covering the distance quickly.

She walks behind, slowing, then stopping. Calling out Nadine's name.

The teenager turns to her, hair spinning as she does. It's beautiful, isn't it?

You go ahead. I'll wait here.

What. I want you to come with me.

Yeah, but. From this distance Nadine already looks like part of the group. You'll be fine.

You're just going to wait here?

She shrugs. Nadine is already starting to walk backwards. She waves.

A boy in a red sports jacket lines up behind Nadine. Then they all disappear inside.

The Courtauld Gallery itself costs eleven pounds to enter. The exhibit rooms have a mild, controlled atmosphere. She laps each exhibit, passing paintings Nadine would recognize, gasp and point at purely because they are famous. She deliberately ignores them. Another visitor stands in front of a painting and sketches it. What is the point, she thinks. Then there is the Manet of the girl behind a bar. Fuck you, Manet. Then the Gauguin of a sleeping girl. Fuck you, Gauguin. An hour passes and she is on the first floor again, finding herself in a low-lit and low-ceilinged room. Religious imagery from the medieval period. The gold leaf dull but glinting still. She slows down then stops before a triptych: Virgin and Child with Saint. The middle image depicts Mary the Virgin sitting upon a throne with her baby. In the images either side, surrounding them: the birth, and the death, of her child. She folds her arms. Points a toe, readjusting her stance. Thinks: God, I am being dramatic.

She finds Nadine sitting on the edge of the fountain next to the boy in the red jacket. Others are surrounding her, framing her: other potential students, people in blazers, people with round glasses.

Nadine's eyeline rises, registering her approach, slack face reanimating and saying, Hey. This is Gabriel. Gesturing towards the boy beside her, who nods with thin eyes. Gabriel already got accepted onto the course. Right?

He nods again.

So why are you here?

Both teenagers glance up at her.

Oh, Gabriel says, tipping up his chin. I just wanted to have another look. I love this place. Indeterminate accent with the American twang.

He's going to help me with my application, Nadine says.

Right. Can we go?

What? No, not yet. Everyone is going for lunch.

We have to get back.

Why.

So I can paint you.

This is the artist I told you about, Nadine tells Gabriel. She's going to paint my portrait.

The boy's expression changes to one of interest. Where did you study?

The Slade, she responds casually, knowing he'll be impressed.

A girl appears and sits down next to Nadine, curling an arm around her neck and handing over her phone to the teenager. Here, put your number in, the new girl says with a clipped posh accent.

Hey, Nadine calls as the girl gets us and heads back to another group. Let me know about that room as soon as you can, okay?

Nadine can survive without her. No – Nadine *will* survive. Her own existence does not come into it. I'm going, she says. You can stay. Although the lighting will be good this afternoon, in a few hours or so. The sun hits just the right place in the sky to give you a glow. What's it called? Turning to the boy. Golden hour?

Golden hour, the boy responds, drawing out the vowels.

Plus it will be raining tomorrow. So as the sun sets tonight, it could turn pink. It will be really beautiful. Obviously that means the lighting will be terrible tomorrow.

Wow, says the boy, nodding.

Nadine registers the boy's approval. Pulls on a sleeve. But these are not her clothes, so the sleeves are not long enough.

Using a chair as a makeshift easel, she steadies the canvas on it. The Golden Hour is elsewhere. The light in her room is dull, nothing glows. The teenager is looking out of the window and not talking. She has been in a mood since they left the Courtauld.

She tries not to acknowledge the absence of something once there. The powerful suck of sinking sand.

I'm almost ready.

The teenager responds, Mmm.

What's wrong? As though anything could be wrong.

I wanted to stay for lunch. They said an important professor might turn up.

She unwraps newly bought paints. You didn't have to leave.

I thought you wanted to help me.

I've given you a place to stay. I took you to the open day. I could even help you with your application, you know. I did get myself into the Slade.

Nadine approaches the canvas and uses one finger to tap on its frame. Her expression is *difficult to read* – just like her father. Your phone is ringing, Nadine says.

It is. A distant thrum from the bed. She picks it up. Gustave. Having unblocked her, apparently. She disconnects the call, replaces it face down and says, So, are you ready to start?

Who was it?

No one.

Now Nadine is looking at her. You're being weird again.

The look is direct. She battens herself against it. What do you mean, *again*?

Nadine shrugs. Sometimes you are just weird. In how you

behave. Like. Like you have a secret. Like you want something and you won't tell me what it is. Or I have done something wrong and you won't tell me. Have I done something wrong?

No, she says. I don't know what you mean.

Nadine's expression isn't anxious or judgemental, but plain concern. For her. You know. Before I met you, everything was normal, the teenager says.

A car horn sounds outside. Once short, and then longer, a drone. One of her hands is shaking. She picks up a paintbrush to busy her fingers. Her skin itches. She waits for Nadine to finish the sentence, or better yet, to look away. Nadine does neither. So she looks away first, pretending to focus on the canvas. Nadine's gaze remains on her. Nothing she can do about it now. Nadine is seeing her. We're losing light, she says.

In the space before her, Nadine begins undressing. Bent, hair falling over her face, one eye glinting at her.

What are you doing?

I want it to be a nude.

She watches the teenager pull off her shirt, her trousers. The clothes become dark, pooling on the laminate. The appearance of paler skin, moles, blonde hairs catching the light. Shadows in crooks, elbows and armpit. Darkness and dark hair. Dry skin on a heel. Fatty tissue trembling with the beat of her body as she moves around. No round belly. The scoop of her breasts. As Nadine climbs onto the bed, elongating, reaching her arms above her head, adjusting, her whole musculature reveals itself. Once she is settled, she averts her eyes to show that she is ready. Her body a fact. The pose her own, comfortable without needing direction. Far more comfortable in her own skin than she is.

She wants to say okay, or something, but everything belongs to Nadine now. Instead she repositions the chair and the canvas and begins.

The sketch is first. She finds that the brush resists her hold. Feels awkward between her fingers. As if she might drop it. She pierces the tops of paint tubes and applies the paint directly onto the canvas, pushing into it, building the body on the surface. The link between the body before her and the secondary form on the canvas guides her like puppet strings.

She captures the turn of the head and angle of the thigh in strokes of white. Each application of paint reveals Nadine, as if she is threading the fabric of her presence into the canvas. And in minutes an image glows there. And the image is hers. The image is hers.

Are you nearly done?

It's still the sketch. She creates a triangle for the dip between the arm and ribs. The influence of a curve.

You can't work faster?

She frowns and moves behind the canvas so that Nadine cannot see her.

Nadine says something else. Then: when are you going to do any sculpting. Honestly. Are you really a sculptor?

And she realizes the teenager is poking at her.

Painting was what I used to do before sculpture. And drawing before that. It's. It's part of the process: making studies, understanding form. You'll learn all about that on your course. If you get in.

Nadine is silent briefly.

Can I see the other portraits you have done?

Other portraits?

Yeah. You told me you find models on the street all the time.

Maybe later.

But where are they? I don't understand.

Could you keep still.

Nadine, having gone to sit up, slides back into her original position. I think I should call my dad.

She is using a brush now, pushing it hard into the canvas. No. It's not a good idea.

What will he do? Now I am here. He cannot force me to come back.

Then what's the point in calling him.

Maybe he's worried.

The teenager's face achieved in a zigzag of red. Trust me, Nadine. He does not want what is best for you. She angles herself around the side of the canvas to meet Nadine's eyes. But the naked teenager is looking down at the pink phone in her hand.

I will just tell him that I'm okay.

She lurches, and she must clip the canvas with her elbow, because it spins on a corner and clatters loudly to the floor. Paintbrushes spill everywhere. Tubes of paint. Nadine looks at her with vague alarm and clutches the phone to her chest. She grabs for it, grasping only the empty air around her. Don't.

Nadine's pupils have widened. But why?

This time she grasps it, the bundle of Nadine's hand and Nadine's phone. Nadine protests, struggling, but lets go of the phone.

At the window, she swings the latch, pulls open the frame. And now the phone is spinning away and into the empty skip below.

She has not noticed the amber in Nadine's eyes before. The flash of it. The teenager looks at the window, mouth open. Why did you do that?

Just let me finish the painting.

What is this? You want to keep me as some kind of prisoner? Nadine's accent is slipping with her fear.

She feels as though she has lost her skin.

Listen to me. Your dad is controlling you. He's the one holding you prisoner. He could give you any opportunity you want.

Why would he withhold that from you?

Nadine's mouth quivers before she starts to speak. Because he's worried about me. It's normal. He's my dad.

Listen, I know more about your dad than you do. He just. Uses people. Uses women. He just strings them along and then drops them when it's no longer convenient. When he has no use for them any more.

What. Why are you saying these things? Stop it. Nadine is shuffling back up the end of the bed. She nears her. Notices how the teenager's skin is turning purplish with cold.

He cheated on Christine, did you know that?

No he didn't. Why are you saying that? Nadine wipes her face with one hand. Stop talking about my dad like this. You don't know him.

I do know, Nadine, I know.

Heavy tears fall down Nadine's face as she pulls the duvet over her head.

Do you want to know how I know? Because it was me. He cheated. On her. With me.

Only the top of Nadine's head is showing from under the duvet, staticky hair.

He started it and then just dumped me. She pokes further. Ghosted me. Whatever. So how can he know what's best for you when he treats women like that? When he has a daughter. When he has you. She realizes she is panting. There is paint water on the floor, seeping into the clothes Nadine shed moments before.

Is this true? Nadine, voice suppressed beneath the duvet.

Yes.

When? Nadine re-emerges, face pink. Sniffing. When?

A sudden regret. She's said enough. Too Much. She backs away from the bed slowly.

Did something happen at his apartment? When I left?

She picks up the chair and then the canvas, the paintbrushes, the tubes of paint.

Well, was it then? What happened? Nadine's face has already changed: a new and naked girl.

No, she responds.

Nadine goes to speak again, but nothing comes out. Her mouth wobbles, nose scrunching. Did you know I was his daughter before? When you found me?

She decides it is best to say no more.

Now Nadine pushes away the duvet and stands by the bed. She is bright and tall. The centre of the room into which all light is absorbed. There is a tear on Nadine's cheek that she has the urge to wipe away with her thumb. But Nadine shoves her aside with both hands and starts picking up clothes from the floor. Picks up the shirt that is not hers, heavy and wet. Tosses it back to the floor.

How did you even find me? Voice angry, shrill, almost ear-piercing. No. No, I do not want to know. I want to go home. She fumbles with her underwear, not crying any more. What did you want me for, in all of this?

You can't leave now. How will you get back?

How should I know? You smashed my fucking phone.

So just stay. She backs herself against the radiator, fingernails digging into palms. Just stay here and we'll figure it out.

NO.

I'm sorry.

I don't care. Nadine starts throwing things into her suitcase. What are you sorry for? For stalking me? For. For using me? *Putain*.

Please. You're making yourself more upset.

Nadine ignores her and stamps into the bathroom, returning

with lotions and plastic bottles she had scattered around the sink. She drops them into her suitcase, stamping everything flat with her feet. A zipping sound – it makes her wince – as Nadine fastens her suitcase.

Now Nadine looms over her. She shuts her eyes completely. The force of the girl engulfs her. What else is a lie? Huh? Would you even like me if I was not his daughter? You know. Nadine's voice is flat. The only true thing you have told me is that you are an artist. That is all that you are.

Her face is salty. She is crying. She hears the door open and hears herself saying, How will you get back? I can come with you. I can help. We are friends, Nadine. I love you.

Nadine has left her hairbrush. It is pink. She picks it up. Pushes her fingers into it. Hooks out a clump of strands. They circle her forefingers. She pulls them tighter, twisting until her fingertips become red, angry, then white. She brings her fingers to her nose. The hairs smell of artificial fruit. She can finish the painting with the memory of the girl.

When her phone vibrates again, there are three missed calls and one message.

Nadine bought a Eurostar ticket on my credit card. Is she with you?
She responds: *Yes, she is here with me.*

What he wants now is a cigarette. He fumbles in his shirt pocket, then an inside pocket of his suit, his trouser pocket, the other trouser pocket, but finds nothing. He swears. There is a great unknown before him. His daughter is not replying to his messages. He has flown straight into an unknown in order to make it known and then to destroy it. These are the lengths to which he will have to go. Past these ugly people and through this ugly town.

The map on his phone leads to a building with a dirty black door. He has thought about this place throughout the journey. What did he expect – an apartment block? No. Something so squalid? No, not that either.

He presses the bell he has been told to press and then she is there. The Girl. Her hair is not how he remembers, cut without style, making her face sharper, stranger. Of course she is one of those crazy bitches who cuts her own hair. And those small eyes, that sharp nose. How did he ever find her attractive. Although her smell has changed, is no longer that sour scent of desperation. There is something else now. What does she know that I do not. What does she have that I do not.

The Girl stands aside, letting him in. He does not obey and waits on the doorstep.

Where is Nadine? he asks. No need to fuck around. No need to allow this girl any control of the situation.

You have to come up, she responds.

This feels risky. He had expected his daughter to appear, to be returned to him without fuss and for them both to return home. But there is more to do, more lengths to go to. He stares at The Girl. God, her face is strange. What is this new feeling?

He steps inside, walking sideways to avoid her, but his chin still ends up stroking her forehead. He is here for his daughter. That is all.

The Girl starts to walk up a set of carpeted stairs. He follows. It stinks in here. It is a dump. He begins to feel assured again. The door to her room is open and he follows her in, registering the smell of black damp, the kitchenette filled with dirty pans, plates, cups everywhere, the cheap fittings. That is the problem with these girls, the desperate ones – they lead disgusting lives.

Nadine, he says, because there is no need to shout. It becomes immediately clear that his daughter is not here. There is nowhere she could be in this tiny room.

The Girl watches him. He is reluctant to ask *where is my daughter* because to do so would acknowledge that she holds the answer. He looks at her in a way that lets her know: You have no power here. Whatever you are playing at, it is over.

Despite himself, he leans across her and looks into the tiny bathroom. Cosmetic pots, bottles on every surface. Overflowing. Scummed tiles. Small bin overflowing with god knows what.

No Nadine. As he had expected but half-hoped otherwise.

There are marks on the wall, plasterwork exposed, scratched at. Why would she bring him here when Nadine is not here. Perhaps Nadine has never been here. Then where is she? Has The Girl brought him here as a trap? He opens the wardrobe. Clothes. All black. He closes the wardrobe.

He looks at her again. That sharp face. Always something behind it, something that – he admits it now – puts him on edge.

Losing patience, he shouts, Where is she?

She's here.

It is only then he notices she is standing in front of something propped up on a chair. The Girl steps to the side to allow him to see it. A large picture. A painting. Shiny, still wet. A body. A naked female body. A young, naked female form. Small breasts, ribs pushing through. Small triangle of dark hair. Horror at the sight of his naked daughter. As though finding her corpse. My girl, he thinks or murmurs, bringing his fingers to the canvas, touching it delicately as though to test an injury. Withdrawing his hand, he sees wet red paint on his fingertips. His daughter's body, now with track marks.

The Girl. When he approaches her, she backs away. But the room is so small that soon there is nowhere left to go. She meets his eyes. Trembles beneath him. At his mercy, her look expectant, worshipful.

What to do with this small and pathetic thing? His hand is clutching at The Girl's middle, the paint from his fingers transferred to her clothes, staining them. She is a mess. Something stirs in him. A pure and perfect urge. She doesn't flinch. Why does she stay put? Why not fight him off?

Buy it, she says. I need you to buy it.

ACKNOWLEDGMENTS

To Lamorna, Damian and Neil at Weatherglass: thank you for pushing me and thank you for making this what it is, James Tookey, Luke Bird and everyone who made this book.

Thank you to those whose conversations, remembered or otherwise, fed into the narrative. Including: the critique of Paris tourists wearing berets – from my Mum and Marnie. And from Pippa: the notion of Becoming Something being so much more concrete upon giving birth, as opposed to being an artist.

Thank you Emma, my eternal art wife. Thank you Moira for the laptop!

And thank you, MD.

HOW TO BE A FRENCH GIRL

ROSE CLEARY

First published in 2023
by Weatherglass Books

001

Cover design by Luke Bird
Typesetting by James Tookey
Printed in the U.K. by TJ Books, Padstow

A CIP record for this book is published by the British Library

ISBN: 9781739260125

www.weatherglassbooks.com

Weatherglass
Books